Her Brother's Keeper
A Murder Mystery

Hollie Tutrani

Dedication

I dedicate this book to my family members who love me unconditionally. My husband, Wayne, read and reread my book and helped me with its historical content. He is my rock and the love of my life. He has always been proud of me and never fails to make me laugh out loud. He is my precious *"Ol' Fossil."*

I also want to dedicate this book to my children, Jill, John, and Staci, and their spouses, Josh, Amanda, and Richard, who encouraged me to write and follow my dreams. They love and support me, and fill my heart with happiness. They have always given me such joy and purpose. I couldn't be happier to have the privilege to be the mother of children so supportive and devoted. I am so proud of them.

Nicole and Deanna were born in my heart, and I love them very much. I cannot forget my grandchildren Sawyer, Anaiah, Rowan, Aila, and a little boy coming in November, who have my heart. I cannot imagine a life without my grandchildren, watching them learn and grow into who they will become.

To Mrs. Brizzie, who always had faith in me and had a lasting influence on me. And finally, I dedicate this book to my mother, Judy, who passed away too soon from ovarian cancer and to those who suffer from postpartum depression.

I wouldn't be who I am today without these people in my life.

Acknowledgment

My husband, Wayne, gave me constructive feedback and advice on piecing this book together. He was the backbone of the process, and I want to acknowledge him for driving my creativity in the best way. I also want to acknowledge all those who inspired me to put my writing skills to the test. If it were not for going through eye-opening experiences, I could have never made the story what it is today.

About the Author

Hollie Tutrani was born and raised in New England. She is a retired police detective, a wife, a mother, and a grandmother. She enjoys reading, especially mysteries, and she always had a vivid and creative imagination and naturally sleuth instincts. She recently discovered her love for writing with her husband.

She enjoys knitting, gardening, cooking, and spending time with her friends and family when free. Mostly, she enjoys playing around with her grandchildren, who call her 'Mimi' out of love. Hollie resides in Florida, where she is a successful real estate agent. She lives together with her fluffy Sheepadoodle, Willow, and Goldendoodle, Cooper. She also has two cats Frankie and Nena, both of whom are a bundle of joy.

Prologue

Hilda felt the warm yet soothing afternoon breeze brush past her face. She stood and faced the sea as the ship steadily moved forward. Her mouth was left agape at the sight of the gigantic Statue of Liberty extending its cement torch upward. Her brown eyes were glued to it.

"Hey, make some room," a man yelled, brushing past her as she stood like stone in his way. The statue so absorbed her that she did not respond. She heard more people flocking beside her and cheering heartily. Her big moment was finally here. She was going to reach the United States of America soon!

The ship arrived at their destination, and she got off, feeling the tremble in her legs. Without knowing a lick of English, how was she to survive? Her parents crossed her mind as she began to doubt herself. She took a step forward. She was anxious about leaving them in Germany on the brink of war, but she still wanted to make the most out of her own life, just for them.

"I can do this…" she whispered to herself and muttered a

little prayer. Was America going to promise her a life full of happiness and love?

Hilda knew nothing of what was in store in the future, but only that this nation was supposedly her haven. Well, was time merciful enough...or was it? She would soon find out!

Contents

Dedication..*i*

Acknowledgment .... *iii*

About the Author .... *iv*

Prologue... *v*

Chapter 1- Germany 1939 .... *1*

Chapter 2- Hilda... *32*

Chapter 3- Sam *39*

Chapter 4- Adal *83*

Chapter 5- Tim.. *121*

Chapter 6- Crash *140*

Chapter 7- Aftermath *155*

Chapter 8- Picking up The Pieces *163*

Chapter 9- Simple Life... *176*

Chapter 10- Farm Day *192*

Chapter 11- Something's Wrong with Colleen *205*

Chapter 12- Married Life *218*

Chapter 13- Sickness *229*

Chapter 14- Tim's Collapse... *235*

Chapter 15- The Big Secret.. *246*

Chapter 16- Murder.. *264*

Chapter 17- Home *287*

Page Left Blank Intentionally

Chapter 1
Germany 1939

In January 1933, Germany elected Adolph Hitler as Chancellor. Humanity was about to enter into a dark chapter in history. It was as intense an atmosphere as any German citizen had ever experienced, ushering in a wave of destruction that none could have predicted.

A war would soon be upon the German people for the second time in recent history. Fate would be rewritten, and the course of nations would be altered. But for one young lady, Hilda, it was the beginning of a new life.

Hilda's mother, Britta, worried – as most mothers did – for her child's welfare. Although they were not Jewish, everyone feared the instability of the new Chancellor. With war clouds looming over Germany, a sense of urgency accompanied her second letter to her sister, Eva, who was living in the United States.

Eva had started a new life in the U.S. over five years ago with the help and support of Britta and her husband, Yusef. She had moved to NYC in search of the 'American dream of prosperity,' a world away from the poverty and uncertainty that enveloped Nazi Germany in 1939.

Somewhere inside, Britta knew that if anyone could understand her desire for the freedom of her daughter's life, it would be Eva. How could she not? Some time ago, she had been there herself. And back then, Britta had not backed away from helping her baby sister realize her lifelong dream of living in America. There was no way she wouldn't do the same for her niece. But Britta's hesitation had a valid reason.

She knew that Eva was not the motherly type, yet she implored her sister to consider taking Hilda in at her home in the States. Not wanting to imply that Eva would have to take care of Hilda, Britta explained in her letter how helpful her daughter could be to Eva, who lived alone in NYC.

Hilda, now 17-years-old, was not a child anymore. She was an exceptional student, a hard worker, and a caring person. Britta did not want her daughter to be compromised due to the war. She had to do everything she could for her beautiful girl.

Britta had to think of a scenario that Eva could not refuse, so she wrote the following in her second letter.

Liebe Schwester,

I hate to write to you again regarding Hilda, but I am desperate for your help and assistance. Germany is going to war. We are all struggling just to survive. Mama and Papa are gone now. The Nazis have seized our farm, and all our money is depleted. We are barely scraping by, Eva. Unfortunately, Yusef was injured in an accident. His spine is fractured, and he has fallen gravely ill. Things are looking bleak for us here.

Hilda is no longer the child you remember, Eva. She has grown into a fine young lady, an excellent student, and a compassionate daughter. What a blessing she has been to us! I can assure you that Hilda will not be a burden to you, Eva. Her dreams will never see the light of day should she stay here with us. I want you to take her in at your place in America. You are the only one I can trust with my daughter's safety. I know I am asking you for a debt I will never be able to pay off, yet I cannot help but ask.

Please Schwester! We are desperate for your help if only just this once. Can you find it in your heart to help us?

With love, Britta.

Britta did not know whether or not Eva would be convinced to take Hilda in. There was no quick response to Britta's second letter. Nevertheless, she held onto hope that Eva was only delaying assessing her own ability to care for Hilda. Her sister was not going to refuse her.

Finally, as Britta had predicted, although begrudgingly, Eva agreed to take Hilda in. It seemed only right, after all, Yusef and Britta had paid Eva's passage to the United States and supported her financially for several years. Now that Eva had established herself in the U.S., she didn't need their support, but they required hers, for the sake of her daughter.

Britta tore open the letter from Eva when she received it. It read:

Dear Britta,

I'm sorry it has taken me a while to get back to you. I really had to think things over. I need to tell you that I was less than truthful in my letters over the years. I told you I was working for a reputable company, but that is a lie. I am also not living in a high-rise apartment in the city.

The truth is that I work all day as a waitress in a diner and as a bartender at night. I live in a trailer owned by the bar owner, and I struggle daily to make ends meet. I'm so sorry I lied to you both. I didn't want you thinking of me as a failure since you gave me most of your savings to come here.

I was worried about how I would manage if I took in Hilda, but I heard the news, and I know I should help. Yes, you can send Hilda here, and I will do the best I can. She's not a child, so it shouldn't be too much trouble. I hope we get to see you and Yusef soon, as well. Please give my love to him and tell him you all are in my prayers.

With love, Eva

Britta smiled in relief after she read her sister's letter. She could sense her sister's reluctance in the letter, but it only made Britta smile even more, knowing how blunt Eva could be. She felt that her sister had forgotten her family, and at times, she seemed too selfish. But Britta could tell from the letter that Eva had a soft spot for her family.

"Hilda! Hilda! Come here," Britta called out to her daughter from the kitchen.

Hilda came towards the kitchen in a rush, bewildered by the look on her mother's face. Her long brown hair was flying as she entered in a hurry. She had been brushing her hair when she heard her mother calling for her.

"What is it, Mama? What's wrong?" she asked. Britta had a subtle smile on her face and gave her daughter a huge hug. "Tante Eva has sent me a letter. She has agreed to take care of you in America!" Britta said.

Hilda paused, unsure of how to react. Was she supposed to be happy or sad?

"I… don't know what to say. Mama…" she stammered.

Britta shook her head, "No, no, no, dear! This is good news! Papa and I will be fine here. We have lived our lives, Hilda. We want you to live freely in America. Wasn't that one of your dreams?" Britta asked in excitement.

"I want to stay here and help you. Papa is sick, and I don't want to leave him…." Hilda trailed off. She was frightened to be anywhere without her parents, especially in another country.

Britta answered, "No, my child, you should go to America. Don't miss out on an opportunity like this. It was quite an effort to convince Eva to take you in."

Hilda gulped. "I do not want to go, mother!" She said, almost raising her voice.

Yusef, hearing the commotion, walked into the kitchen. There was a time when he was a strong man of military bearing. He used to appear tall with sharp, well-defined features. But now, he was a broken soul. He couldn't stand straight or walk without a cane. He was only in his forties but looked so much older.

"What's going on?" He asked them. Hilda pursed her lips tightly, refusing to talk. Britta stepped forward to help her husband sit down.

"I received a letter from Eva. She's agreed to take Hilda in!" Britta informed with a smile. Yusef's face lit up. "That's great news," he beamed in a raspy voice, before lapsing into a coughing fit.

"I don't want to go," Hilda whispered as she took her father's hands in hers. "I want to stay here with you. I can't bear to leave you alone in such a condition," she said. Tears were pooling up in her eyes.

Yusef shook his head and gripped her hand tightly. He said, "Please. Please don't say that. You must live on! There is nothing here for you."

Hilda was not hearing any of it. "I want to stay here! I want to stay with you, papa. Why are you sending me away? Don't you want me here?" She began to cry.

Glistening tears rolled down her cheeks. Gently, Yusef wiped her tears with a wavering hand. With a soft and tired smile, he said, "We love you, Hilda. That is why we are sending you away. We want you to be safe and have a chance to live a great life."

He stared at his daughter, who still seemed stubborn. He explained, "It would be much harder for us if we had to worry about you while going through the conflicts in this country. There is no future here in Germany. Please, do this for me, if not for yourself, Hilda," he begged.

His answer was so sweet and straightforward, Hilda felt the truth behind those words.

She had great respect for her father. Hilda hugged her father tight, and so did he.

Within the next week, Britta helped her daughter pack. Mixed feelings flooded her heart and mind. There was more than a good chance that they would never see her again. She was sending her only daughter to a faraway country, but there was no looking back.

Britta had to focus on the future. She knew Germany was destined for war – the signs were unmistakable. Her daughter had to leave; the parting would be painful but it was for the best. Unlike Germany, America was a land of opportunity and freedom.

It was better for Hilda to be in America than to endure yet another war as she had. Soon, there would be nowhere to run in Germany. America was the future and the only choice. Even if Eva were living in a trailer and working in a bar, at least the Gestapo wouldn't barge in and tear their family apart.

Eventually, Hilda also began to embrace the idea. She had heard all about the land of opportunity, despite the talk of a 'depression.' What did that even mean? Hardship? "Germans know hardship, let me tell you that," Hilda thought. She had always dreamed of living in a faraway land, free to explore and express herself, like every teenager. It would be a wonderful musing.

Hilda felt her place was at home, helping her mother and father and enduring hardships together. She knew they would shelter her for as long as possible, but the time for change had to come.

Hilda was a smart girl, and she was aware that Germany was headed for war. In her heart, she knew her parents were doing the right thing. But it was scary, too. She hadn't seen Eva since she was about eleven-year-old. She wondered what it was like in New York City. It was exciting yet frightening all at the same time.

Hilda had never been on a ship before. It was overwhelming in every way. "Enormous!" was the only word Hilda could find to describe it. She exchanged a tearful goodbye with her parents, and off she went. Hilda was embarking on a new life, just like that. Third class tickets were in no way luxury accommodations, but she had to manage. The repulsive smell of rats and sewage made her gag every day. The rocking of the ship was also maddening and made the five-day trip absolute hell.

Finally, the journey came to an end. Someone called out, "Hey! We are approaching the symbol of freedom, the Statue of Liberty! Look at her!"

People aboard cheered and cried at the sight. Hilda felt like doing the same. The tall, beautiful lady standing gracefully, welcoming them to America was a breathtaking sight. Hilda was in awe. She smiled as her heart leaped with joy.

After processing at Ellis Island, a grand way station that was the door to America, Hilda found her way to the ferry. Then, she went to the train station as she was instructed. It took a long time as there were thousands of people. There were so many people speaking different languages. It was an exhilarating experience for her.

As Hilda boarded her train, she remembered when she would dream of an exciting new adventure in her life. She dreamed of travel, opportunity, and, lastly, the freedom to express herself. She prayed that America was everything she wanted. The train screeched to a stop.

Hilda had arrived at her station. She stepped out onto the train platform and was greeted by masses of people everywhere. Where was her aunt? How would she find her in this crowd? After scanning and searching the public over and over, panic began to set in. "Am I lost?" Hilda wondered.

She heard someone call out for her amid the noise, "Hilda, Hilda!" someone shouted. It was her Aunt Eva. She emerged from the crowd, wearing a red dress that stopped just above her knees. She wore black stockings underneath, that highlighted her long legs. The dress accented her aunt in a way that warranted many stares.

Hilda became self-conscious, as she was wearing clothes that one could only consider dull and worn out. Her dress was a plain gray that fell to her ankles. Hilda was suddenly unsure of how her aunt would react to seeing her.

Eva surprised Hilda by engulfing her in a tight hug. "Welcome to America, dear! My, have you grown!" she said excitedly, and smiled, "I'm sure you are tired. Let's get going."

Eva spoke those words in perfect English. Hilda was amazed by her fluent English. Hilda was fluent in English and German, Hebrew, and French, but she never spoke as clearly as Eva did. Eva's heels clicked their way across and out of the station. "Taxi!" she yelled.

A lemon-colored taxi stopped in front of them, and the two young women entered without a moment's hesitation.

Hilda imagined that her aunt lived in a large home with a front porch, garden, and a gorgeous backyard, just as she had seen in the magazines and newspapers. She couldn't wait to see it. NYC was beyond beautiful with high buildings, busy streets, and all these delicious new smells.

As they rode on, the scenery began to change. The buildings were gone. The lovely homes vanished as the road went on. It looked like they had exited the "nice" part of NYC.

Eva lit up a cigarette. Tendrils of smoke rose, hiding her face for a brief moment and filling up the taxi . Hilda choked as the fumes blew onto her face. Her nose scrunched, seeing her aunt take long drags from the cigarette. She waved the smoke away, not trying to hide that she hated it.

"Where are we going?" Hilda asked.

"Home," Eva responded.

Just as she spoke, the taxi turned into a rundown trailer park that looked like a junkyard to Hilda. Broken-down cars dominated her view. Laundry hung off the rusted porch railings, and trash of every kind carpeted the streets. Stray cats and dogs roamed everywhere.

The taxi stopped in front of a dark and dank looking trailer at the end of the road.

"It's not much of a house, but it's clean and affordable," Eva said sadly. Hilda's image of the skyline view of Central Park with a rooftop garden shattered to pieces.

"Tante Eva, I thought perhaps you had settled down with a husband, and you were..." Hilda was at a loss for words.

Eva sighed, "No one wants to settle down these days, Hilda. The depression has been hard on families. And with Germany invading Poland, well, let's say that ruined Germany's reputation here.," Eva sighed.

Sadness took over her. "Anyways, I need to go to work. No matter how poor, people will find money to drink at the bar. I also need to pay the bills," she said.

"You are going to work dressed in that!?" Hilda blurted out without a thought. She inspected the dress closely and saw that her aunt had no corset under her silky red dress. Hilda instinctively covered her mouth with both hands.

"Oh, man!" Eva giggled at Hilda's disapproving stare.

"Men pay for their drinks and then some, Hilda. They pay a little extra for a show..." she winked.

Eva turned back to add, "Oh, and only speak in English, please. It'll be better for you, trust me."

Hilda only nodded. The Eva she remembered in Germany was just as bubbly and carefree, but she was now what...a prostitute?

Before leaving for work, Eva gave Hilda a tour of her new cramped living quarters. Hilda thought the place was ugly and depressing from the outside. Everything inside was disheveled but somewhat clean.

"Not clean like mama's clean," Hilda spoke out in a whisper to herself. It smelled of stale smoke, which made her heave a sigh. Her father smoked a pipe. Hilda liked that cherry tobacco smell, but he never left an ashtray full like this. "Mama would clobber him," she again whispered to herself.

"Not what you expected, Hilda?" Eva responded to Hilda's whispers under her breath.

"I had written to your mother and explained. Didn't she tell you?" she asked, but Hilda didn't hear her at first.

She was busy staring at the broken window boarded up with cardboard. A blue davenport was covered in newspapers and there was a tiny kitchen sink with two plates, two mugs, and a spoon inside it.

There was also a small stove with pans on top, their arrangement announcing the lack of space. The place was so cramped that Hilda wondered if the two of them would fit in there at one time. This seemed like a nightmare.

She asked, "How will we fit?"

"We will manage, but you will have to help out," Eva quipped.

Hilda merely stared at Eva who sighed and began, "I have a life that is not conducive for a child. I can't have them around. But Hilda, you are seventeen. So, I expect you to use common sense, and you know…"

Staring at her with piercing blue eyes, Eva exclaimed, "Welcome to the real world, Kind."

'Kind' meant child in German. Eva weaved in some German for Hilda who still looked shocked. She expected the home and lifestyle that Eva had written in her letters – the skyline apartment with dreamy views of the Statue of Liberty and fancy furniture. She wondered what happened to all of that.

Before Eva left, she let Hilda know that she had made her dinner. "I hope you like it. Get some rest, we have a big day tomorrow," she chuckled.

Hilda politely thanked her aunt as she placed the utensils in front of her. Eva turned toward the door.

Hilda stopped her, "Wait! Aunt Eva? Where will I be going to school?"

Hilda loved school. She was great at studying, and was especially good at mathematics and reading. She loved reading but many books were burned and banned in Germany. Now that she was in America, she hoped to discover all the reading material the country had to offer. Despite the initial shock, she was now excited about her new school.

"Yeah, I have made all the arrangements for you. We will settle it all tomorrow. That's why it's a big day!"

Hilda grinned in response, and a look of excitement came over her face.

"Can you believe that there are no uniforms in the schools here, Hilda? So odd!" Eva added.

Hilda opened her mouth to answer but Eva cut her off, "Anyways, I'm running late. Goodnight!" She waved and went out the door.

"Goodnight, Aunt Eva," Hilda replied.

It wasn't that late, but Hilda ate and then decided to go to sleep. It had been an exhausting trip. Also, she knew she would have to face her uncertain future head-on in the morning.

Hilda slept on the davenport on the first night in her new home. The stiff fabric chafed against her skin and she couldn't find a comfortable position to rest. It wasn't exactly what she expected but she would make do. Slowly, her eyelids drooped from exhaustion, and she drifted off to a dreamless sleep.

She awoke to a bright sunny morning. Eva was already up, making breakfast while smoking a cigarette and holding a coffee mug in her hand. "Good morning. Did you sleep well?" Eva asked.

"Yeah, I was so tired," Hilda replied.

"Coffee?" Eva offered.

The two sat down on the davenport to catch up on family over coffee. Eva had missed most of the changes in Germany over the past five years. The conversation only made Hilda miss home. It was only a small house in which they lived, but at least it was tidy, and she could call it 'home.'

Hilda thought about her mother's cooking. She would decorate the table with biscuits, marmalade, and a slice of ham and eggs every morning. Thinking about it, she could almost smell the meals her mother so lovingly prepared.

Her parents would always wake up hours before Hilda to tend to the chickens and other animals outside. Her father would milk the cows and slop the pigs. They always waited to eat breakfast until Hilda got up, so they could start the day off together. Mother had biscuits and ham precooked and warmed in the oven. She would set the table before heading out.

Hilda never thought much of all they did until now. It had been rough on the family emotionally when their farm was seized. Food wasn't as readily available, and her father had to work in the garage, fixing cars and trucks to earn money.

They moved into a flat above the garage. Her father began to get sick every day. Under the Nazi Regime, medicine was controlled by Berlin, and it was nearly non-existent for common folks. So, he just had to do without it.

Hilda hated working in the garage with him. But now, she thought she would rather be there than sit in this shabby place. At least, she felt provided for and safe there, even if it was a flimsy sense of security.

She hoped that coming to America wasn't a mistake. Now, only time could tell whether this was a mistake or a great decision.

"I promised them I'd be helpful to you and become a successful woman," she told Eva.

"Then you better find a rich man to marry!" scoffed a cynical Eva.

Although America was not at war, there were signs of it everywhere. People were glued to their radios, especially listening to Edward Murrow. America was a melting pot of all cultures, so everyone there had relatives in other countries. War was imminent! It was the talk in every barbershop, diner, church, and house. Schools even had drills.

Within a week, Hilda was enrolled in school and was now attending her first day. It wasn't easy adjusting as a new student because she was a senior in high school. She tried her best to stay optimistic, but she would soon learn that fitting into a foreign culture would take time.

However, time was not on Hilda's side. As Germany invaded Poland, American resentment for Hitler and the Nazi's multiplied.

In general, the Americans were not interested in another European war, but that sentiment was about to change. There was no escaping the fact that Hilda was German. Her accent, dark brown hair with natural red highlights, and European features were hers to own. Some of the kids were friendly at first, but most were not. They were emptying the fear within their households onto Hilda.

As the months passed by, Hilda had to endure some horrific abuse. She was called all kinds of names, many of them being Hitler lover, Nazi, and other displeasing names. She tried to explain that she was not a Nazi and that she was here to learn to be American. The insults and teasing became a constant source of anxiety and stress for her. She cried herself to sleep night after night.

She always pondered to herself, "Perhaps, if I just became invisible, the other kids wouldn't notice me."

It was just a silly thought. It didn't work. She was pushed, tripped, and hit... and continued to be called all types of names. The bullies would shout at her, "Go back to Kraut land, you Nazi!"

It just kept getting worse. Eva had little to no maternal instinct, but she tried to advise Hilda on dealing with the bullying.

"Just don't pay any attention to them," Eva would say. She tried spending some time with Hilda to comfort her. It seemed to help at first.

Hilda was lonely at school, and the only kids that would even talk to her were social outcasts like her. Smoking and drinking were how they dealt with the stress and pain of rejection. Hilda refused to be crushed by such harmful coping mechanisms.

Perhaps, if she could change her look and appear more American, like actresses Rita Hayworth or Greta Garbo, it could reduce bullying. She cut her hair so it fell to her shoulders and curled it with hairpins. She wanted them to look like Rita's curls.

A little makeup wouldn't hurt either. It took her a long

time to get it right. Hilda washed off her first few attempts after staring at herself in the bathroom mirror – all unsatisfied. But she was determined to get it right, and she did with the help of her two friends, Colleen and Meg.

Colleen Kelly and her two brothers were orphaned as children when their parents died in an accident. Her older brother Jason later joined the Army while she and Tim continued to live with their widower grandfather on his farm in Tarrytown, New York.

Colleen didn't have a mother figure either. She was a determined, get-what-I-want type of girl.. She was no pushover and would set anyone who came her way straight. Nothing ever stood in her way. She fought for the underdogs and never judged anyone.

Hilda and Colleen hit it off, and became great friends.

On the other hand, Meg Foley was the good girl of the two. Her mother was involved with the local church PTA and city council. Her father was a detective for the New York Police Department and worked directly with the Commissioner. He was a very important man and rarely home because Mayor LaGuardia was trying to clean up the city. The murder rate was high in the city, and Detective Foley was a stellar and dedicated homicide detective. He worked round the clock like most detectives. Meg also had trouble with her peers in school. She had been very shy and was often teased. She would just take the teasing and then cry in private. Hilda and Colleen stood up for her, and there was an instant connection.

Meg and Colleen managed to endure the pressures in school somehow, but Hilda had reached her breaking point. Hilda was now eighteen and failing her classes because she couldn't concentrate on her studies. She just couldn't find a reason to continue anymore.

She decided to drop out of school during her senior year. She always felt lonely and depressed even at home, and pondered what future America could offer her. She always questioned if she would ever be able to go back home to Germany. She missed her father with every fiber of her being. She was the center of his world, and he was hers. They were inseparable, especially when he wasn't so unwell.

Hilda was very studious and had a huge heart. She was a pretty girl too, and many young lads had set an eye on her. She sure missed that. In America, she had no one except for her two friends whom she didn't meet regularly. She was alone and angry for being deceived and charmed by the 'American Dream,' which didn't exist.

Where was this welcoming, beautiful America that Tante Eva wrote to them about? Where were all the nice things America had to offer? She didn't know what the economic depression had done to the States. But she thought about it all, "At least, I don't have to beg for food, medicine, or have the Krauts kick open the door and tear up my floors as they did in Germany."

Eva was anxious after seeing Hilda's condition. She tried to convince Hilda to stay in school, but to no avail. In some vain attempt to give Hilda a ray of hope, Eva blurted out, "Why don't you come work with me at the bar? You will just get bored of doing nothing, Hilda. There's no other work for us at the moment, and this will help us get some money to drink."

Hilda decided to accept her aunt's offer, "Fine. When do I start?"

It surprised Eva, but with Hilda's current state, it was likely she would have agreed. Hilda was out of options. She was smart and young. She had so much going on for her, but she could not see it now. Her self-confidence was bruised. The world around her seemed to be filled with so much hate. Everyone was suspicious of everyone.

Hilda began to work at the bar. She had become used to her aunt's flirtatious personality, but she found it to be quite educational in itself when she experienced it firsthand. She quickly learned how to bat her eyelashes at the men seated, show a little leg, and put on just enough to show that she might attract a larger tip. Each night after the bar was closed, Eva drank with her after-hour crowd.

Eva told Hilda that this was where the big tips came from, "Drink with them, give them attention, and see how fast their wallets open."

Through slurred speech and breath that reeked of gin, Eva declared, "All is lost. Look at us, Hilda. We can still cut a rug. We're young and..." She hiccupped out loud. She covered her mouth and pushed a bottle of Gin toward Hilda, motioning for her to have some.

Hilda refused even to try. Her aunt's complete loss of dignity was embarrassing, but Eva was persistent. Hilda did witness those wallets open with her aunt's skills. She worked at a bar now. A little booze wouldn't be the end of the world.

She took a small swig and spat out the liquid all over Eva, who didn't seem to notice, strangely. "Here, try again. It's easier the second time," Eva laughed out loud.

This time, Hilda swallowed the vile liquid. Immediately, she yelled out for water, "Widerlich! Wasser!" Her cheeks flushed, and her stomach was burning. After a couple more gulps, she was overheated and lightheaded and leaned on the bar. She tried to compose herself.

The after-hour boys laughed. "Hit 'er up again,'" they chanted. She swore she would never drink like her aunt, but that promise was short-lived. Eva said, "Honey, this is an answer to your sadness., Drink up, and take a break from all the crap that you've had to put up with."

That sounded lovely to Hilda, so she drank and laughed. Then, she gulped the alcohol again and laughed some more. They danced and drank more until she was flying in her head. The results that evening were predictable! When morning finally came, Hilda's head throbbed badly, and her stomach ached from retching all night.

Eva, on the other hand, showed no ill effects from her indulgences. Her body had become immune to alcohol's deadly effects. Hilda slowly embraced Eva's destructive habits instead of turning away from them. The two bonded with the foggy haze that drinking produces as well as common sadness.

Hilda still hated it. She didn't like the taste of alcohol but liked that she could forget everything, even for a few hours. She could forget the school that she loved and forget the home she missed in Germany. She forgot her father doting on her, and her mama's knitted sweaters and home-cooked meals. She drank to forget it all.

Hilda had no problem getting Colleen to join in. Colleen knew how to have a good time. She was always ready to listen to Hilda and let her pour her heart out. Colleen seemed to know just what to say to make Hilda feel better. She and Hilda became inseparable. They wanted to bring Meg out of her shy shell, but that was no easy feat.

Meg was a church mouse. She was such a good girl that Hilda sometimes thought she was a bore. Colleen managed to get Meg to drink on a few occasions. It was somewhat funny because all she did was giggle. When she drank, she opened herself up to new adventures. Hilda wasn't sure it was a good thing or not. It only took one drink or two, and Meg would collapse and want to go home.

Hilda often envied Meg. She had everything Hilda ever wished to have. Meg still lived with her loving, doting parents, and she worked at the church library. Colleen, on the other hand, lived with her brother and grandfather on a farm. Hilda loved her life back in Germany and would do anything to go back to those days.

Colleen said she hated the smell of the cows and the noise of the pigs and chickens. She couldn't wait to move back to the city where she lived before her parents died. She loved her brother and grandfather a lot, but she found farming a total bore. Colleen was quite the character. She was always up for an adventure.

Hilda became popular with some of the regular customers. Their comments about her being 'pretty' or a 'babe' found a home in her lonely heart. Hilda began to smoke and drink like Eva as an attempt to blend, and she did blend! She soon had trouble even remembering who she once was. She used to be a loving, compassionate daughter and an 'A' student. All of it was now only a distant memory.

Hilda wondered what her parents would think of her. They would most likely be ashamed. This was the reason Hilda avoided writing back to them, even though she had received a few letters to date.

She just could not lie to them. So, she didn't write back at all. Eva was growing quite anxious the more she watched Hilda degenerate into well... herself! She had ruined Hilda, and now, she hated herself for it.

One night, Eva confessed to her companion for the night about her distress. "I have so messed up," she said. A handsome man in his mid-forties sat next to her on her bed and politely listened as she rambled on in her drunken stupor.

"Mike? It's Mike, right? I never wanted kids, you see. Now I have this teenager who was dumped on me by my sister. I never planned on living for anyone but myself. Do you understand? It's my sister's fault, isn't it?" she asked.

He nodded in agreement. Eva leaned over and kissed the man, "Make me forget about all of this for tonight, will you?"

Together, they fell back onto the bed. There was no one

to interrupt them. Hilda had stopped returning to the trailer for some nights to give Eva her privacy. She stayed in a room above the bar, weeping over everything that had gone wrong.

Chapter 2
Hilda

One thing Hilda knew for sure was that she had no desire to spend her life serving tables or scrubbing dishes. She hated it all. It wasn't the life she ever wanted for herself. If she did, she'd have preferred staying in Germany.

At first, Hilda was demotivated and couldn't imagine a prosperous future for herself in America. But the more time she spent at the bar, the emptier she felt.

After months of working there, Hilda realized that she indeed needed to do something with her life. This realization didn't hit her like a ton of bricks, all of a sudden. It built up bit by bit. The resentment inside her grew.

Hilda was driven by this anger to achieve success. She imagined a life where she would provide for herself. That would be her way out of this mess. Hilda was not to repeat the same mistakes that her Aunt Eva continued to make. Somehow, she knew that throwing herself at men would not produce the results that she craved.

She wanted to be somebody. She hoped to be successful, but she needed to get hold of some money and develop a plan. While maintaining her job at the bar, Hilda decided to work extra days at a local catering hall with Colleen and Meg.

Although Hilda didn't make it obvious, she was a little envious of Meg. Meg had a supportive family. They encouraged her to seek new opportunities and helped her with whatever resources they had. They were also kind-hearted people, only wanting the best for their daughter. Hilda tried not to think about it too much. When she did, her heart rate would shoot up, and an unswallowable lump would form in her throat.

Meg didn't stay in Hilda's life for long. She left for California to go to a secretarial school. However, Colleen stayed behind, and she and Hilda took on as many shifts as they could at the hall. They both worked hard to earn money. They decided they would save up, open a dress shop in the city, and share an apartment.

Hilda was finding new ways to improve her appearance and become more attractive. She put a lot of effort into choosing pretty clothes, makeup, and jewelry. She also managed to help Aunt Eva with the expenses at home to the best of her ability. Eva was as lost as ever. She never seemed to realize that she needed to love herself before loving another, a lesson Hilda could use herself!

The year was January 1941, and things were changing. President Roosevelt entered into a Lend-Lease agreement with the U.K., the sole holdout in the Nazi Blitzkrieg that had engulfed most of Europe. In need of desperate support, Prime Minister Churchill had struck a chord with FDR. As Congress debated the bill, an opportunity was about to present itself to Hilda and millions of other hardworking Americans.

New jobs opened up at the newly activated military industrial complex in Brooklyn Naval Yard, but Hilda found she wasn't eligible for it, being a German national. .But when one door closes, another opens.

For Hilda, the exodus of workers, male and female, heading to the naval yards, opened up more opportunities for additional days and shifts at the catering hall.

As Hilda began to make some extra money, her concern and guilt at practically abandoning her parents began to eat away at her. She decided to send weekly letters to them. Her parents didn't have any money when she had enough to spare.Her parents rarely responded, so Hilda was seriously concerned about their health and well-being.

Once, when Hilda did receive a letter from her parents, they had returned the money she had sent. They had no way of converting U.S. dollars into their currency. This made her feel even more helpless and guilty.

The one letter that they sent after a very long time read:

Our Dearest Hilda,

You've grown into a fine young lady. Your father and I are very proud of you. We are doing as well as expected, so there is no need to worry, my dear. We will be just fine. We see you are doing well in America. Thank you for the money, but we cannot exchange it here, so we have sent it back. You should put it to good use and buy yourself something nice. We love you till our last breath.

All our Love, Mama and Papa!

The thought of her parents enduring such hardships was weighing down on Hilda.. As her parents chose not to align themselves with the Nazis, work was undoubtedly scarce to non-existent. Mama never mentioned anything about that, but Hilda wasn't ignorant to what was going on in Germany.

She was always glued to her radio like everyone else. Many people talked about the war and believed the United States would be involved in it soon enough. People didn't trust each other because the U.S. was a country of many nationalities. Who was who? What side were they on? The fear of the communist party was still everywhere since the first war.

She felt so lost. There was plenty that her mother never told her, and this was the one thing that made Hilda quiver in fear. Her heart ached for family and she longed to go home. Distance had created a deep yearning for home in her. She missed everything about it – even the things she had never liked. She remembered a much simpler life. The farm with chickens, pigs, and one crazy rooster that just couldn't get his timing right...

She reminisced about sitting by the radio with her mother and father. The golden-red fire in the woodstove made the room cozy. Mama was knitting, and Papa was smoking his pipe. Hilda even longed to go back to her school and complete her homework by the fire. But that was no longer a reality.

Nothing could replace the loneliness that Hilda felt. It was like a deep vaccum – an open mouth of isolation that she feared would swallow her whole. She would do anything for a hug from her parents. Every time she saw ordinary families chuckling, hand-in-hand, her heart broke into pieces. She was her father's pride and joy. They used to do everything together She missed him terribly.

Yet, she had to find a way to stop feeling sorry for herself because no matter how difficult Hilda had it in the U.S., her parents were enduring worse hardships.

She did have at least one good news in her life. Colleen got married to her short-term boyfriend, John Logan. The couple discovered Colleen was pregnant so they married right away. John was in the army and ready to deploy while Colleen moved into a city apartment. She still worked to pay the rent. With the marriage and the baby, their dress shop plans didn't seem to be working.

On the other hand, Hilda's constant desire to succeed was being polluted with Eva's suggestion that she must 'meet and marry a wealthy man.' Hilda thought that each new man she would spend time with would surely be the one to rescue her from a life she hated.

But her dreams never materialized. Instead, those relationships would always end the same way with Hilda feeling completely worthless, used, and discarded like trash.

Left with an insatiable need for love and attention, Hilda wanted the love Mama and Papa had always given her.

Chapter 3
Sam

The grand ballroom parties introducednew opportunities to Hilda. She worked hard and kept her eyes and ears open. She enjoyed these parties. She imagined herself as a debutant, linking arms with some wealthy man. She wanted love, but she was more than ready to settle for riches.

Saturday night was another fancy party as far as Hilda was concerned. This one was thrown by a man that owned most of the city. As Hilda prepared for the evening's event, she was in awe of the room's ambiance.

There were carpets with extravagant floral prints, chandeliers that sparkled like diamonds, candles on every table along with pink carnations, and musicians sporting black and white tuxedos.

Seeing such a lavish party was a bit worrying if you looked at the economy's condition. This money could feed a lot of people. But this was work, and that was what she needed to do. There was no need for any extra thoughts.

Then, as if fate had called out her name, Samuel Granger strode into the room. He was tall and dashing. He sported a double-breasted navy pinstriped suit and black leather oxfords.

She got to know that Samuel Granger was a wealthy builder and business owner from Westchester County. This evening's Gala was held to celebrate all of his hardworking partners and their companions. All the proceeds of this party were supposedly going to feed the hungry.

Women strode in, placing an elegant hand on the arms of handsome men. They were dressed in furs, dripping in jewelry, and exuding an air of elitism. Hilda had never seen such beautiful dresses. There were some down to earth people there, too, but Hilda didn't even notice. She was caught up in the glitz.

After a few more minutes, she heard a voice addressing the crowd, "A toast to all my friends, associates, and their families. As tough as this year has been, we find ourselves here tonight, having conquered every obstacle that has beset us. Let us raise a glass to success, my friends, and our generous pledges."

Samuel Granger had quite a way with words. Hilda felt blood rush to her cheeks, hearing the man's deep and charming voice. Everything about him oozed confidence, but he belonged to the world of glamor, while she was only a low-wage worker. Their worlds would never coincide.

All of the guests replied with a, "Here," as champagne glasses clanged, followed by conversation. Hilda was smitten. She imagined herself beside this magnificent man, and for just a moment, she was blind to everything else.

"Hilda? Hilda? Where has your brain run off to?" Her name was spoken in a soft tone across the room. Hilda was still in a daze till Colleen tapped her shoulder, "Where is your brain, Hilda? I have been calling you!"

Hilda, who usually worked harder than any of the other waitresses, was at a loss for words. "Table 2 needs coffee,. Hurry, please," Colleen scolded as she carried out two pots of hot coffee for other tables. Hilda hurried over but realized that she needed help. She called out to Meg, who had recently come home from California and rejoined the trio.

"Help me clear this table, and please bring out the dessert," she informed. Meg obliged. Hilda juggled dishes and empty glasses, stacking them on a tray, and rushed toward the kitchen. Once there, she saw that Colleen was up to her old tricks again. She was poking fun at all the guests, imitating their high-minded looks and social graces.

Her jokes just tore the kitchen up with laughter. Hilda deposited the tray with the dishwasher and was laughing hard. She proceeded to step back into the ballroom, but her foot wobbled. It seemed that she was about to go on a date with the floor, but fate intervened, and she fell right into the arms of that handsome man who had caught her eye earlier. He was now holding her.

"Ah, mein!" Her German slipped out. She silently cursed to herself. In front of Hilda stood a man of great stature! She guessed he was over six feet tall with broad shoulders and the softest brown eyes she had ever seen. He had a neatly trimmed beard, which made his sharp jawline look even more prominent.

Hilda was embarrassed. If he reported her clumsiness, she could lose her job. Yet, all Hilda could think was that this man was the most handsome, no, gorgeous man she had ever seen. Their eyes locked. Hilda blushed, then as if being awoken from a dream, she remembered to apologize.

"I am so very sorry, sir," Hilda said.

"No need to be sorry. It was my fault anyway," replied the baritone voice of Samuel Granger.

Hilda melted inside. Her heart was thumping heavily, and she almost broke into a sweat, staring at the man. "What was this feeling?" she wondered. Her entire body reacted to the sound of that deep voice. It was a feeling like warm water was being poured slowly over her as she blushed from head to toe.

"He's an American," Hilda thought to herself and blushed once more, remembering her poor English.

"Is there something I can get for you?" Hilda asked him after adjusting her hair, which became messy from the fall.

"I was just about to try one of those crackers…Miss?" His voice trailed off in a questioning tone. Hilda saw that he, too, was blushing, which made her even more nervous. "What's your name?" he asked.

Hilda was alarmed that he wanted to know her name. Afraid that he was about to report her to the head staff, she averted her gaze. Sam sensed the fear in Hilda's eyes, so he put up his hand to comfort her.

"Oh, I'm not asking you, so I can complain, I was just curious. My name is Sam Granger, and I would like to know the name of the woman in possession of such beauty."

Sam picked up her hand and brought it to his lips while continuing to stare into her eyes. His partner, Brent Parente, laughed as he elbowed Brian, Sam's investor. Sam gave them the look. Brent's wife, Melissa, kicked him under the table.

"What!" Brent cried out to Melissa, who just rolled her eyes.

"Let him have his moment, she's quite lovely," she whispered in his ear.

"But 'possession of such beauty,' so sappy, don't you think?" he whispered back.

"Look and learn, darling," Melissa joked.

Sam's little brother Zeke encouraged the teasing from Brent. Melissa just shook her head, "Incorrigible, the lot of you!"

They were the people closest to Sam. It was thrilling for them to see he had noticed such a pretty woman. All Sam ever did was stay buried in work.

Hilda was oblivious to the whispers behind her. She was speechless at the gentlemanly act. She had seen this before, but it was usually reserved for the privileged class. Hilda was nothing special and wondered why he would even take a second look at her. Sam's words were consuming, and when Hilda heard the word 'beauty,' she blushed very hard.

Hilda became self-conscious about the way she was dressed. She wore a plain gray dress with a starched white apron just like all the other catering staff. Somehow, she found her voice and answered, "I'm Hilda Taylor."

She refused to use her German name and told him the Americanized version she had adopted from a past associate. Hilda slowly withdrew her hand from Samuel but couldn't shake off the shy intimidating feeling that had come over her. This was not her. The Hilda she knew was a strong and feisty woman. All of that had flown out the window. She melted at the sight of this gorgeous man who locked eyes with her.

She somehow found her voice again, "I should get back to work now." She attempted to push past him, but Sam gently gripped her hand, not forcefully, but firm enough to stop Hilda in her tracks.

"At least, allow me to have one dance with you before you leave," he asked her softly. Hilda's jaw dropped. Things like that never happened to people like her. "Me?" she said incredulously.

Sam just looked at her and grinned, "Of course, who else would I be asking while holding your hand?"

She was smitten by Sam but afraid to lose her job. She quickly looked inside the kitchen and saw that no one was watching. They were all busy. Hilda did not have the willpower to refuse him.

Sam led her to the dance floor. Immediately, they were pierced by indignant and disgusted looks from Sam's 'friends.'

"Just look at her," one of them said aloud. Then, whispers began to fill the hall.

"Who does she think she is?" another scoffed. Some said perhaps Sam had an escort for the evening. Indignation and rage dripped from their entitled lips. The voices eventually reached Hilda's ears.

Hilda's face was flushed. She felt the blood rise to her head from hearing all the condescending comments and ruthless stares. It was challenging to endure it all. Hilda was more than aware that they were a mismatched couple at best. She was in her servant's frock while Sam was dressed to the nines from head to toe.

Hilda was happy that she had taken a little extra time to curl her hair and adequately applied her makeup. Her beauty was apparent to all who stared at her. So even with that frock, she knew she looked better than most of those pompous prigs. However, she knew he was out of her league.

When Hilda fell a step behind, Sam commented, "What's the matter?"

Hilda started to say, "I don't think..." she stopped and began to look at every one individually. Sam only gave her a soft smile.

"Forget what they are saying," Melissa reassured from the side. "Just enjoy the dance," she smiled.

Hilda's lips shook to find the right words, but she noticed Sam staring at her intently. He seemed love-struck. He gazed into her beautiful eyes, porcelain skin accenting the golden flecks in her deep brown eyes. He was close enough to notice the small beauty mark above Hilda's upper lip. Sam had romanced quite a few women in his day, but he had never been this intrigued by one. He could tell that Hilda was unlike the others.

He hadn't missed her lilting German accent. Her childlike face and innocent, doe eyes were enough to bring a smile to his lips. He was drawn to her from the moment he laid eyes on her. It was strange, but he wanted to keep Hilda close to him, even if the disapproving glares detered him. It was quite rare for him to feel instantly connected to someone.

He asked, "I haven't seen you here before Hilda," as they swayed across the dance floor. Every woman in the ballroom was green with envy. And why wouldn't they be? Sam was a prized bachelor, but right now, he only had eyes for Hilda. Sam continued to ignore her lack of dancing skills and took charge of the dance, supporting her with each step.

Hilda finally got the courage to speak, "I have only recently started working here. I'm from Germany…" her voice dropped to a whisper. She was feeling unworthy, which was a most definite attempt to sabotage this moment. Sam seemed not to care at all that Hilda was from Germany.

"A beautiful country, Germany. My father took my brother Zeke and me there when we were boys," he said.

"It is quite upsetting to see what that evil Chancellor is up to. Europe has seen this type of aggression before. So very sad! I believe the United States wants to be neutral, but I will fight for this country if I have to. This is the greatest country in the world," he added.

Hilda pursed her lips. She did not want to talk about this. Her parents were still there, and Sam quickly got the hint after seeing her uncomfortable expressions. Gracefully, Sam shifted the moment back to dancing, twirling Hilda and dipping her low.

"Well, I'm glad you're here now," Sam said.

"How old are you, Hilda, if I may ask?" Sam asked, suddenly thinking she might be too young for him. Not wanting to spoil the moment, Sam held her close and twirled her around twice.

Hilda was too afraid to answer him. He was so dreamy. What a terrible question for a girl to have to answer!

Smiling shyly, she answered, "I've just turned 19."

Sam exhaled in visible relief while maintaining an entrancing eye-contact with Hilda.

"I'm almost 26. A….bit too old, you think?" he asked playfully.

Hilda shook her head and winked, "Maybe.". Her confidence was coming back.

They both chuckled.

They danced for a while, smiling at each other with love dripping from their eyes. Sam squeezed her hand all of a sudden and blurted out, "Let's go for a ride."

"A ride?" Hilda replied.

"Yes, this place is too boring," Sam said.

"But I have to work! I can't…" she started, she looked back at the kitchen and saw Colleen and Meg waiving her out of the door.

"We have this, go!" they mouthed.

"No worries, I know the owner well," he winked. Hilda grabbed her bag and Sam draped his camelhair overcoat around Hilda's shoulders. She was still taken aback by the interest Sam showed in her, but she felt drawn to him, too.

She didn't want to dwell on the reason too much. If it was love at first sight, so be it.

They both walked out; the lot attendant quickly brought Sam's 1940 Lincoln Continental convertible around the corner. It was black with thick white-walled tires that practically disappeared under the enormous rear fenders. The sideboards and chrome shined as if the car was brand new.

Hilda's eyes practically bulged out of her head. Sam opened the passenger door for her. She slid in, grinning from ear to ear.

"I take it that you like the car," Sam smirked.

"I've never seen a car like this before," Hilda exclaimed.

Sam noticed Hilda's excitement, so he told her all that he knew about the car and why he had purchased it in the first place. He'd bought the car a year ago. Earlier, he had a rusted old green pickup truck, but his friend Giuseppe owned a Lincoln dealership in New Rochelle and gave him a price he couldn't refuse.

"You are never going to have a nice girl in that ol' truck of yours," he had told him.

As much as Sam hated to admit it, he did love the car, but he hated spending money on himself when others needed it more. Giuseppe's business had hit hard times lately due to the economy, and Giuseppe was a hardworking man from Italy who provided for his wife, mother, mother-in-law, and five daughters, all in one house. Sam felt for him and bought the car and paid the full price.

"I'm glad I have this car tonight," he beamed.

Hilda was at a loss for American words, so she just nodded to his words. He laughed, finding her naivety to be adorable.

"Want to see something crazy?" Sam asked suddenly.

Hilda shot him an eager look. "There is more to this car?" She questioned under her breath. Just then, a whirling of a motor could be heard. The car's top retracted, exposing them both to the cold night air.

They roared in laughter. Hilda, let out a "Swell!" as her smile lit up her face. She stared up at all the twinkling stars as Sam drove up the Hudson River on Route 9A.

"What a sight!" Hilda exclaimed, watching the lights of NYC becoming smaller and smaller behind them. The beauty of the Hudson River shimmering in the moonlight left her speechless.

The leaves had turned into hues of magnificent deep orange, red, and yellow. The moonlight made some of them look like stained glass. It was beautiful! Hilda insisted on keeping the top down, even as the cold air of the late September evening nipped at them both.

Sam gave Hilda his hat, gloves, and scarf just to keep her warm. Hilda felt on top of the world. With the wind passing through her cocoa-brown hair, she laughed innocently.

In that instant, their eyes met and felt as if they could drown in each other's lustrous orbs. Was it love? Hilda was sure this man held a special place in her heart. She knew the feeling was reciprocated as Sam leaned in to give her a peck on the lips.

He dropped Hilda off at the trailer park where she lived. He didn't question her place of residence, nor did he care where she lived. Sam was down to earth and humble despite his riches. He was a man of honor and truly cared about people. He did all he could to help the unfortunate of the world.

Sam didn't care about money, but he had plenty of it. He gave away a lot of it. So, whatever roof was over Hilda's head didn't matter to him. All he knew was that Hilda was radiant and astoundingly captivating, and he was in love. He didn't voice his thoughts out to Hilda but hoped she got the message.

Hilda, on the other hand, was disappointed that her utterly romantic evening had come to an end. But before she opened the front door, Sam asked her, "When can I see you again, Hilda?"

"Tomorrow night?" he added.

Hilda's heart skipped a beat. He reached forward and pulled her close, kissing her on her cheek. She blushed as blood rushed through her body like it did the first time. "Tomorrow....7: 00 p.m.," Hilda said.

"You better not be late."

As his car roared away, Hilda floated into the trailer to tell her aunt all about the beautiful evening that she had just experienced. Eva thought Hilda had gone mad, though the gorgeous convertible parked outside the trailer had not escaped her attention. You wouldn't see such cars often in that neighborhood.

Hilda could not wait to share the night with Meg and Colleen. She called Colleen,

"Operator? Give me plaza 345…Colleen...yes, I know the time. Yeah, it's late, but I need to tell you about my dreamy night! Well, first we…"

They chatted for hours. That night was only the beginning of Hilda's love story. Sam spent the next few months taking Hilda out on dates and showing her all that society had to offer. He understood that she had never been exposed to such things, and he just adored seeing her face light up with excitement.

Sam and Hilda went to museums, shows, clubs, movies, and of course, they dined out. Sam spoiled her as much as he could. Whatever she wanted was hers!

Hilda no longer needed to fantasize about living a comfortable life; she was experiencing it firsthand. Sam began calling her "His Hildie" affectionately. She loved the nickname more than anything and always persisted him to call her by it. Eventually, Hilda, with Sam's insistence, quit her job at the catering hall, later to find out that Sam owned it.

Hilda had never felt so alive. She thought about Aunt Eva's words, "Marry a rich man." She was living the dream, but she never thought she would fall in love with that man, too. She had it all. It was surreal that all that she had ever dreamed of was right before her eyes.

Colleen and Meg realized that this was Hilda's chance to change her life. Hilda began to rely upon Sam for everything. As the months passed, their love grew, and they melted into each other. They had dinner, danced, and flirted on romantic nights almost every day.

Through Sam's help, Hilda even went to Frank Sinatra's concert. She was in the front row. The movie shows that she saw with Sam were just stunning. Gone with the Wind, The Philadelphia Story, and The Grapes of Wrath all left Hilda speechless.

Sam was a true gentleman, and Hilda was deeply in love with him. Instinctively, Sam knew how to satisfy her insatiable need for attention. Sam had never seriously considered a committed relationship until now. He told her about his previous relationships and how he never loved a woman earnestly. But now, he found himself thinking about a family with Hilda.

It was hard to believe that they had been together for nearly a year.

Sam knew that Hilda had serious insecurities, but he also saw a strength in her that even Hilda didn't know she possessed. He was slowly being exposed to her uncanny talents, for instance, her ability to repair autos, a skill she learned from her father.

She showed her impressive skills once again on one occasion. They were out on a Sunday drive when Sam felt the brake pedal going too low. Something was not right.

Sam was a man of many things, but a mechanic he was not. He pulled over to take a look, but it was Hilda who jumped out first. In a flash, she popped the heavy hood of the car and began working on the cause of the leaking brake fluid.

Hilda assured Sam that she could fix the problem. Sam chuckled but declared that he was going to get help. He bounded down the road towards the nearest garage. Thankfully, his mechanic Griff's garage was close by. He reached it quickly and started looking for Griff.

When Griff came, he immediately told him the problem and asked him to come and inspect the car.

When they returned to the car, to their surprise, they saw Hilda behind the wheel smiling back at them. Griff inspected her work and nodded approvingly at Sam. He gave the nod to Hilda, as well.

"Where did you learn how to do this?" Sam asked. Hilda gave them both a coy look and said, "Back home in Germany, I worked with father."

Sam couldn't stop smiling. After Griff left, they talked about her past.

"Yusef…papa, back in Germany, made the decision to resist the Nazi party in 1936. I was a young girl then. Nazi's burned our family farm and looted everything we had because of this decision. Work became nearly impossible to find. Not being a party member was not an option for most German citizens. We didn't have much, but we had each other," Hilda choked back the tears that her memories evoked.

She continued mixing English with her German accent and said, "Papa made ends meet by using his mechanical skills on the rural farms where we hid. We were surviving until he became injured in an accident when a car slid off the lift and crushed him. His back was never the same again. It was then that I started helping him with the mechanical repairs, eventually taking over for him. It was about this time that Mama decided to write to my Aunt Eva and inquire about sending me to the United States."

Hilda's teary eyes met Sam's. Sam held her hand tightly and said, "Well, I, for one, am glad that you are here."

"Me too," Hilda replied. The mood was grim till Hilda nearly jumped out of her skin when Sam tossed her the car keys and informed her that she was about to learn to drive. She was absolutely giddy as a little child on a Christmas morning. Hilda jumped into Sam's arms, "Thank you for everything that you've done for me," she exclaimed through the widest grin Sam had ever seen on her face.

Hilda showed him she already knew how to drive. It was at that moment that Sam realized he should never underestimate her determination. With each passing day, their love grew. She had said she wanted a 'rich man,' but she was surprised that she loved Sam with all her heart. She knew she would still have been head over heels for him if he didn't have a dime.

Sam, who had fallen in love with Hilda's beauty, now admired more of her characteristics as they came out. He was attracted to her contagious laughter, wit, innocence, and her strong desire to learn and succeed.

Hilda was a complete package. She was petite yet strong-willed, driven, and ambitious. She was also sweet yet always ready with a sarcastic comment or two, romantic, sassy, and sexy…..he found no flaws in her.

However, Hilda harbored insecurity that Sam would wake up one day and cast her to the side for one of the socialite women in his circle. What she didn't fully understand was that Sam was not like most men, who liked the candy on the arm but wanted to marry a girl like mom. Sam had no interest in the social life of society. He was putting up a façade because of business, and Hilda knew that, yet her insecurities gnawed at her.

She mistakenly took his conservative approach as rejection. Never once in all their days spent together had

Sam ever pursued Hilda beyond a passionate kiss. Hilda wondered whether Sam found her somehow, undesirable since every other man she had dated before always made the first move. Gathering her confidence, she asked him one day, "Sam, do you truly find me attractive?"

Sam simply replied, "Hildie, of course! Why do you question it?"

"You don't seem to want me…you know…" she said.

"I want to cherish our time together and allow things to progress naturally. I just want to enjoy the journey with you," Sam reassured.

He was a total gentleman. Hilda was floating on a cloud, hearing Sam's heartfelt words. He had assuaged her nagging fear of rejection, and at the same time, elevated her self-esteem. Was it possible to feel better than what she did right now? She doubted it.

Eva had her doubts about Sam at first, thinking that he was only going to take advantage of a poor and naive young girl, but as time went on, she changed her mind. He would always bring a bouquet whenever he picked up Hilda. It was a warm-hearted gesture but proved useful in gaining Eva's trust.

Sam had done well for himself despite the congenital disability that left him deaf in his left ear. His parents, Charlie and Annabelle Granger didn't believe in the "poor me" attitude. They treated Sam like he was not handicapped at all. His father was the local butcher in New Rochelle. The business was simply called "The Butcher Shop."

Charlie was a generous man, almost too generous. He often gave away more than he earned. He told Sam and his brother Zeke, "A man isn't a man if he cheats another or eats like a glutton when others can't eat at all." Even during the agonizing period of the Great Depression, they always managed to have just enough to survive.

"That was because doing right always rewards itself," Charlie would often say. He taught his boys to work hard, be generous, help those in need, pay their debts, and love their country.

Charlie took part in the first war and didn't regret his decision. He was more than ready to dedicate his life to the country. He was a great father. When not working in the shop, he did handy work around the house or at someone else's place.

Sam would be right beside him, helping him out and learning from him in the process. Zeke was good with numbers. He studied hard. Sam's mother, Annabelle, would be busy with sewing and doing the laundry while Zeke would hit the books. Zeke would eventually work with Sam to build the business.

It was the good principles taught by their father that made Sam and Zeke the respected men of the community. Sam's business often required putting in extra hours late at night and constant networking. It consumed a lot of his time. He had little desire for the politics of the day or petty arguments that surrounded them. Sam just did what he thought was the right thing, just as his father had taught him.

However, the winds of war in Europe were not so easily ignored. The debate about America entering the war raged all across the political spectrum. Lines were beginning to be drawn. Sam was a patriotic man. He was well informed about the crisis and wanted to do his part.

The America First Committee had none other than Charles Lindberg leading the charge. One European war this century was enough to ask the Americans to sacrifice for their country. This war didn't require America's intervention.

However, Franklin Delano Roosevelt, America's 32nd president, seemed to have other plans in mind. He harbored no illusions that Britain would not survive much longer without being hung precipitously on the U.S's involvement. It was June 1941; the debate was over.

Sam kept his nose down, his pencil sharp, and a fedora on his head. He continued to portray himself as an accomplished gentleman and successful businessman. He felt that if America does go to war, he at least wanted to do his part by keeping the jobs open and helping those in need. He continued to help his community with food and clothing drives.

He helped keep roofs over people's heads, just like his dad did. The thoughts of starting a family with Hilda began to occupy his thoughts again.

***

It was hard to believe that they had been together for a year now as they met each other in the fall of 1941. This weekend was to be special. Hilda was turning 20, and Sam had a plan in mind.

The day began with Eva preparing a pancake breakfast and topping it off with a candle for Hilda. Hilda laughed as she made a wish and blew it out, smiling warmly at her aunt. The two of them seemed to have found peace with each other.

Eva was delighted that her niece had found true love. Hilda was relieved that her aunt had stopped binge drinking and wasn't beating herself up over her decisions like before.

Sam, true to form, drove up at precisely 11:30 am for the birthday plan. They drove for half an hour, off to unknown adventures, at least to Hilda, they were unknown. They stopped at Fifth Ave and 53rd 1069 street, and a horse and carriage awaited them.

Hilda gasped, and her eyes opened wide in surprise. She couldn't explain her exhilaration. She had wanted to go on a carriage ride through Central Park since she first arrived in America.

The air was clean and crisp; just a touch of nip could be felt. Hilda climbed in the carriage with Sam. There was a light blanket to cover their legs. The smell of chestnuts roasting over open coals of the street vendors floated through the air. It was all truly magical.

The carriage came to a stop beneath an enormous elm tree, just before the bridge underpass. Hilda saw a blanket stretched out with a picnic basket to her left. There were rose petals scattered all over the area, and the Sun shone brightly, its light spilling onto the calm riverbed and creating unique patterns. Still, she couldn't put the pieces together.

Sam helped her down and led her to the inviting, romantic scene. Before Hilda knew what was happening, Sam dropped to a knee and said, "Hildie, my love. Marry Me."

Hilda stared at Sam with elation. She was at a loss for words. Sam repeated, "Marry me, Hildie." There was no hesitation in his second attempt.

"Wha-What?" Hilda said. The moment was making her emotional. Sam gently touched her cheek, gazing deeply into her beautiful brown eyes. His mere touch made Hilda's stomach flutter.

He said, "I've never felt more alive than when I am with you. Say yes, my love. I am afraid someone else might snatch you away from me."

Hilda just stared without uttering a word. Sam got nervous when she didn't say anything, but she couldn't. She just couldn't believe that he was proposing to her. She held his gaze, so lost in the moment that she almost missed his gentle hand sliding down deep into the pocket of his Mohair coat, producing a bright red leather box. Sam placed it in the center of Hilda's palm.

He slowly opened the box. Still, Hilda remained silent. Her thoughts were impossible to read, so Sam wavered in his confidence momentarily. Again, he said, "Be my wife, Hildie."

Unknown to Sam at the time, the sheer brilliance of the diamond and rubies had stolen Hilda's voice. She found the gold setting on the ring to be beautiful beyond words.

"Y-y-yes..." she said, barely vocal.

Her eyes twinkled, and she beamed a smile. "YES! YES!" Hilda cried, clapping her hands, and finally finding her voice. She fell into Sam's arms. They kissed with such passion that it stole her breath away. Hilda was crazy with happiness. She simply couldn't believe it.

Suddenly, she drew back with a frown, "Wait, you forgot something shiny!"

Sam laughed, noticing the playful look on Hilda's face. She snatched the red box that was now in Sam's hand and took the ring out.

"Hey, give me that!" Sam laughed. He slowly took the ring out and slipped it on Hilda's finger. It was electrifying for both of them that they were now officially engaged.

"Oh, and happy birthday, doll," Sam said softly as he kissed her again.

Hilda smiled wide, "I can't wait to show Colleen and Meg! They will die when they see this!"

This was the best present Hilda could ever have imagined. No one could have predicted what the next few months would bring. Hectic wedding plans were put in place as Sam and Hilda wanted to get married in December and then have a honeymoon at the Niagara Falls. But when Sam's friend Brian learned of the engagement, he proposed they choose Florida, which was warmer.

Both Sam and Brian worked on several joint projects across the East. Sam focused his efforts on New York developments, while Brian specialized in Florida developments.

When Brian heard of Sam and Hilda's desire to tie the knot in December, he insisted they stay as long as they wanted in his oceanfront beach house on Flagler Beach. They decided to take up his offer. The wedding was all set to take place on Friday, December 5, 1941. Westchester Country Club was the chosen venue.

The thought of marrying the love of her life was enough to leave tingles down Hilda's spine. Still, she was also saddened by her inability to reach her parents in Germany. She wanted to share this fantastic news with them so badly. She had been unable to contact them for the past six months. No mail was getting through as Europe was at war, and the Nazis had ceased all forms of communication.

Still, Hilda had to stay strong. Her big day was drawing close, and she couldn't afford to frown under her pearly-white veil. Her parents wouldn't want her to look sullen on such an important day anyway. The wedding itself was so much larger than Hilda could have ever imagined. Countless well-wishers surrounded Sam and Hilda. Sam introduced her to many friends and business associates.

Even on such short notice, Sam personally invited everyone he did business with. He wanted all of his associates to see his new bride. She had met some before like the Hampton's crowd; the Alberts and the Grabowski's, the Gleason's and the Gauthiers, The New Port RI crowd; the Andersons, the Parentis, the Kalogridis's, and the Cosmos.

They were all willing to travel large distances to see Sam finally get married. Local families like the Wise's, the Fox's, the Miller's, the Stiegler's, the Reiher's, the Yamilkoski's, the Duffys, the Walcots, the Jennings, and the Castagnas were also there.

There were many more from all parts of his life. Eva, Colleen, and Meg were the only guests from Hilda's side. Sam didn't have much family himself. He only had his little brother Zeke, but he was rich in friends.

Sam knew Hilda wanted the wedding to be small, but he made it a dream for her. The venue was the Biltmore Room at the Westchester Country Club and seated 350 people. He was thankful that this room was available since it was so close to Christmas, and everyone was running to book their parties or events.

It was mesmerizing with the pretty rose tones, crystal chandelier, and stunning terrace. The wedding planner, Tammy, didn't miss a beat. There were deep red roses and evergreens at every table, layered in silk and lace cloths.

A 20-foot Christmas tree stood in the corner where the wedding gifts were placed. The tree was colorful with large bulb lights and tinsel that complimented the room beautifully. Hilda wore a long, flowing white gown with beauteous, snowy lacing and a matching train. It was long-sleeved with pearl buttons all down the back.

The bodice hugged her tiny frame. She carried brick-red roses and evergreen in her bouquet. Everything was going well until she had to walk alone into the room. This made her miss her father very much. Her parents would have loved to see this day. She closed her eyes for a moment and pretended that his father was there. Mama was crying, as she would have been, in the front row next to Eva.

She felt their presence even if it only lasted for a few seconds. Sam greeted her in the center of the room. He couldn't believe that she looked even more beautiful than she did every day. The orchestra music played all night, champagne flowed inside gleaming glasses, and exquisite food was served. It was a memorable night. Sam and Hilda were now husband and wife.

The day after the wedding, Sam and Hilda flew to the warm land of Florida. It was the first time Hilda ever boarded a plane, and her stomach was turning. Upon landing in Daytona Beach, Sam and Hilda were met by the finest car service that Florida had to offer.

Then, after a short 30-minute ride, they reached Flagler Beach. Ocean waves and the endless beach greeted them. Their honeymoon was luxurious in every way. There was champagne on ice, gourmet chocolates, and strawberry ice cream, Hilda's favorite.

Rose petals were strewn across the bed, accompanied by two matching bathrobes with the words 'Husband' and 'Wife' thoughtfully embroidered on each.

Hilda was visibly surprised by all the arrangements and couldn't stop smiling. 'I must give him more business,' Sam thought to himself when he saw the look of pure joy on Hilda's face, gazing at the amazing scene before her.

Though their lives were flowing smoothly, it wasn't the same for the rest of the world. December 7, 1941, was a day that would live in infamy. The Imperial Navy of Japan launched a surprise attack on the U.S. naval base located in Pearl Harbor in the Hawaiian Islands.

The loss of life was immense. America was not at war with Japan or Germany. A peacetime attack was simply unthinkable. President Roosevelt was to address the nation about the suddenly ensuing chaos.

Sam and Hilda heard all about the commotion as newspapers were being thrown about. The newsies yelled, "Read all about it! The United States attacked! We're at war! Get your copy here!"

People were shocked beyond comprehension, including Sam and Hilda. America was going to war. The President made it official the next day with a joint declaration of Congress first against Japan, and then three days later against Germany.

The honeymoon was over. Sam and Hilda caught the next flight back to New York. They headed for Sam's Westchester home and prepared for all that was to come next. America's call to arms happened quickly. All eligible men and women aged 18-45 were called upon to enlist. The peacetime draft had already been initiated in 1940.

It was horrible, but the war that Americans thought was far from them now stood face-to-face. Hilda didn't want her husband to leave her, yet there was nothing that she could do about it. She couldn't convince Sam not to join the military. He was patriotic and understood the role he could play in making his nation victorious. The next day, Sam, along with tens of thousands of patriotic Americans, stood in line to enlist in the U.S. armed forces.

Hilda was by herself, worried that she had just married, and now Sam was leaving. The entire nation braced for what was to come next. Sam felt it was his duty and honor to serve his country. However, he was rejected for active duty. 4F was the classification the Army designated, but unbeknownst to Sam, he had a substantial hearing loss that the Army believed to be congenital. So, he would not be going off to war.

Hilda was relieved, to say the least, but Sam was conflicted. All his friends and employees were saying goodbye to their families, while he would remain behind. Sam knew that there must be a way to assist in the war. He committed to doing all he could for his country.

Just when tension lingered in the house, Zeke pulled up in his old pick up.

"Hey, Zeke! Stopping in for a beer?" Sam yelled out from the enclosed front porch.

"Nah, just came by to bid farewell."

Sam knew. He immediately stood up and let the newspaper fall from his hand to the stoop. "Oh..." he choked as Hilda walked out on the porch with her piping hot coffee. It was cold outside. It felt like it would snow soon. The sky looked gray and heavy, but not as heavy as Sam's heart.

"What's this? You are going on a trip, Zeke?" Hilda asked.

"No," Sam spoke softly, holding back tears.

"Zeke's going to war," he sighed.

Zeke stood there on the driveway and said nothing. The three didn't speak for a good minute until Zeke broke the ice, "Its cold here."

Sam chuckled, "Oh yeah, well, are you coming in? Or are you going to stand there and freeze?"

Sam opened the door for him. As Zeke walked in, Sam whispered in his ear, "I'm proud of you, little brother."

With a shaky hand, Sam pulled him into a hug. They hugged it out while holding in their tears. It was unsure when they would meet each other again.

Zeke sat at the table next to the potbelly stove on the porch. Hilda poured him some hot coffee and went to her room to let them be alone. Zeke looked through the frosted windowpane. "I think it'll snow soon…" he mumbled.

They talked for hours. They had a good belly chuckle reminiscing the past with each other. They laughed at all the memories they shared together, but they were still on edge. There was a frown creeping on their faces as the time continued to tick away. Finally, Zeke rose from his seat and said his goodbyes and tearful, 'I love you.'

After Zeke left to serve the country, the reality of this terrible war hit Sam hard while Hilda was concerned about a few practical things. Sam's home in Westchester was an average size for a small family, but well below what Sam could actually afford to live in. Hilda appealed to Sam for a larger home, though the timing just seemed all wrong. They were, after all, living in a country that was now at war.

Many Americans could barely afford to eat, let alone dream of living in large houses. Strangely, Hilda seemed oblivious to the suffering that was all around her. It wasn't as if she didn't notice the atrocities around her, but she didn't want to let it all get to her head.

Sam, on the other hand, seized on the opportunity to help his employees in any way he could. He donated heavily to charities and war bond efforts. Newly formed 'Gold Star' families – those that would lose a loved one in the war effort – would soon benefit from Sam's many charitable contributions.

Sam saw no reason to consider buying another home. This house was enough for him. The view was astounding as the house was set high upon a hill that overlooked the Hudson Valley. Even skiers could be seen in the distance during the fall foliage. It was all absolutely breathtaking.

New York City was also less than an hour away, so what more could one ask for? In the end, Hilda begrudgingly agreed that the house was not all that bad, even though it was much smaller than she wanted it to be. The home was a scant

2,200 square foot; Colonial built in the 1700s. It retained much of its original charm, and Sam loved this home, despite knowing that he could afford one many times larger.

The interior of the house had recently been decorated with new furniture, as well. Sam agreed that Hilda could decorate the house any way she saw fit. This was a way for him to make it up to her as he had asked her to live in this house till, at least, the time was right to purchase another.

Hilda took the role of rich Sam's wife quite seriously. She furnished the home with the assistance of Haversmith's furniture store's interior designer. After much pleading and financial compromising, Sam was able to convince Hilda that modern chrome Formica would not go well for their house.

Sam still felt Hilda's choices were extravagant, but if she was happy, he was satisfied. Hilda hired a housekeeper and a cook. She was wasting no time adjusting to a grand lifestyle.

The war dragged on. It spread from Sicily to Italy. The news was terrible for the Allied troops. Sam lost friends and acquaintances, and he also feared for Zeke. There was no news or updates from him. The war was picking speed, and there was a concern that this might not end as expected. Germany and Japan were proving to be formidable enemies. The 'Gold Star' families were indeed piling up. Sam participated in the war effort and worked hard, be it through recycling metals, bottles, papers, or arranging food drives. Hilda also went along with him and lent him a hand when needed. They were a great team. Despite the war, the first two years of their married life had been truly glorious. Sam demonstrated just how much he adored Hilda. He had to stop showering her with gifts, as Hilda learned the art of spending money all by herself.

Sam spent more time in his office and worked hard for his charitable commitments. He still felt guilty that his younger brother was risking his life on the frontline, but he was not. Hilda helped him with his tasks but not like she used to. He missed his time with Hilda, even though he just couldn't leave work to the side. Sam made a point of telling her just how much he was missing her. He wanted her to come along with him again to collect metal and newspapers for the drives. However, one night as they lay curled together in bed, Sam apologized, "I'm so sorry that I have been spending most of my time at work, my love. It's time that I would prefer to be spending with you."

Sam's heart was sinking, but Hilda's response was mild.

"It's alright, Sammie. I know that you will make it up to me, so I don't mind too much." Hilda had spoken off-handedly. Sam thought her nonchalant response sounded selfish, as if she didn't care if he spends time with her or not.

Sam realized she was quite oblivious to his needs. He wanted to discuss this with her, but she reached up and kissed his lips. He responded immediately to her touch. Her hands seductively caressed his chest. They made passionate love, kissing deeply between soft moans.

Sam enjoyed ravishing his beautiful wife. Their love made him forget what he actually wanted to say to her. All the while, Hilda wondered if this would go on forever.

Everything felt so right. She had everything her heart desired. Sam made sure of that. It just couldn't get any better for Sam and her. She felt cared for, just like when her father used to dote on her with all his time and energy. However, having a husband all to herself was even better.

Life can, however, change quickly.

Hilda had felt nauseous in the morning for a few weeks now. This morning, the same sickening feeling took over her again. She had puked almost three times now, but her stomach still hurt, and the dinner she ate last night rose to her throat. She stared at herself in the bathroom mirror. The woman staring back at her in the reflection had a horrifying look on her face.

'It just can't be. It can't be,' Hilda thought and gulped anxiously.

"Sam," Hilda called out from the far side of the house.

"Yes, my love," Sam said as he quietly awaited her response. He heard nothing, so he got up and walked into the bathroom.

He saw Hilda sitting on the floor propped up against the bathtub with a stunned expression on her face. Afraid to step forward, Sam asked, "Hildie, what is wrong? Why are you sitting there like this?"

The terrified look on her face only deepened Sam's concern. Hilda looked like she would start crying at any moment. She was clutching her forehead, rocking back and forth. Finally, she whispered, "I'm pregnant, Sam," she said so lifelessly that he thought he misheard her.

"What did you say?" he asked with concern.

"I'm pregnant," she said, slightly louder this time as she slumped against the bathtub. Hilda sat on the floor, unwilling to believe it, but Sam was overcome with joy. He stepped forward, knelt down, and pulled his wife gently toward his chest.

"Really?" Sam beamed. Hilda nodded as a lone tear flowed down her warm cheek. Sam missed the clue and mistook this to be Hilda's emotional response to finding out that she was going to become a mother.

"I can't believe it! This means I'm going to be a father! We're going to have a family, Hildie. We're going to have a family!" he rejoiced.

Hilda didn't want to rain on his parade, but she felt numb and anxious, knowing that she was pregnant. Sam's radiant smile was as beautiful as the spring flowers blooming in many hues, but tears were streaming from Hilda's bloodshot eyes.

Chapter 4
Adal

"I hate you! You will never touch me again. You hear me!" Hilda screamed at Sam as she was wheeled to the delivery room.

It was finally happening. The pain intensified with each passing second as the contractions became stronger. She wailed loud enough to startle everyone in the maternity wing. The pain was consuming her from the inside out. Her vision was blurry. She sobbed and screamed for this tormenting experience to just wrap up already. Sam tried to calm her down.

"Oh… God, make it stop! Make it stop! Lass es aufhören!" She begged Sam through her tears. Seeing her writhing in pain, Sam's heart thumped painfully in his chest. "It will be okay, Hildie. It will be over soon," he reassured.

"I don't care! Just make this stop." Hilda choked out as another bout of contractions squeezed her insides. She was going into the delivery room any minute. Sam would be pushed out to the expectant fathers' waiting room. At that moment, all he could think about was the joy he felt when he discovered that Hilda was pregnant.

Sam knew that pregnancy had been tough on Hilda, but he could never grasp the pain and sickness she felt every day. She cried often and hated feeling sick all the time. Not to mention, she was getting fat with the passing months. None of her clothes could fit her at all. Her bladder was working overtime, as well.

People continued to tell her how beautiful the journey to motherhood was, but Hilda didn't see what was so extraordinary about it. She hated being pregnant. It was just a loop of being constantly tired and bloated....she just hated it.

The fact of the matter was that Hilda didn't want to become a mother. Sam found this difficult to swallow. He had been in denial about this from the very moment Hilda discovered that she was pregnant.

Hilda hated how people always gushed at this news with their cheesy, sweet smiles. She would receive a 'congratulations' everywhere she went. They constantly reminded her of something she was trying desperately not to think about. Lost on Hilda was the simple fact that men were dying by the thousands overseas, so what was wrong with celebrating a new life?

Once she became pregnant and the months passed, Hilda realized that her life was changing. She hated that. She felt trapped with all the boundaries that her pregnancy placed on her. The pain and nausea she suffered every day did play a part in making the pregnancy challenging, but there was one more reason why she didn't want a child.

She dreaded how it was no longer going to be about Sam and her. She was not interested in sharing Sam with anyone. He was already bonding with this baby. That was only adding to Hilda's insecurities.

When Sam didn't understand Hilda's attitude toward the pregnancy, he once asked their housekeeper Mrs. Brizzie about it. She told him that some women get baby blues when they're pregnant. It wasn't something to worry about. After spending months with his pregnant wife, he was sure this was much more than the blues.

"Oh, God! Oh, God! This hurts! Get it out!" Hilda continued to scream in pain. She was in a labor room surrounded by shell pink and baby blue walls that were supposed to soothe her. Yet, they only made her more anxious. Pain ripped through her body with such power that she felt as if her body was tearing apart from the inside out.

"Give me drugs!" Hilda begged the nurse who was constantly checking her vitals.

"Something is wrong!" Hilda insisted. "Nothing should hurt this bad! Oh, God. Doctor, get this thing out of me right now!"

Another cramp ripped through her body, contracting her muscles harshly. Hilda shrieked. Tears rolled down her face. At one point, she felt she couldn't breathe at all. The nurses surrounded Hilda, seeming to overcrowd her space. "Get away from me!" She wailed at them.

Her painful screams could be heard outside, and they left Sam worried and restless. He told himself that it was the pain talking. Hilda was just in too much agony to care about what she was saying. Her screeches pierced his ears, but he promised Hilda that he would not leave her alone. So, here he was pacing around the room while Hilda called him every name in her vocabulary.

Hilda had been in labor for just over nine hours now, and there was still no sign of the baby. Sam was worried like most new fathers. Why was this taking so long? Was everything alright with the baby?

A whirlwind of questions circled Sam's head. As he paced around in the men's waiting area, nurses would come out occasionally to inform the fathers to be, who all looked like they could use a very stiff Scotch.

He entwined his fingers and bounced his leg impatiently, waiting for it all to be over. His Hildie had changed, and he knew it. She had grown cold and distant over the past months she was pregnant. He knew the reason. He knew it wasn't baby blues.

They no longer cuddled in front of the fireplace as they did before. She would leave the house without telling him where she was going and would not return until bedtime. Most of his nights were spent sitting alone at the dinner table. He worried about his pregnant wife. He didn't like the way she had grown so distant.

Now that Sam was alone with his thoughts in the waiting room, he contemplated over the past nine months with Hilda.

Those months were absolute hell for both Hilda and Sam and the people around them. Their love was supposed to bloom like a flower on a spring day now that they had a mini version of themselves on the way. But that love continued to wither away.

Sam had tried every trick in the book to appease his wife. He gave her flowers and tickets to NYC shows. He even took her to see the latest Rita Hayworth movie. She was Hilda's favorite actress. Hilda had seen every movie of hers without fail.

Sam tried anything that might allow his Hilda to return to her warm and loving ways. Sadly, nothing seemed to work. After a while, Hilda would go back to her miserable state and end up crying as always.

She would shop for useless things to occupy her mind. Sam expected that she would show him an item that she had purchased for the baby after her shopping sprees. But sadly, that never happened. Not once did Hilda buy anything for the nursery. All she got were useless, expensive items for herself.

It annoyed Sam that Hilda never once bought clothes for the baby. She was not showing any maternal instinct toward her child; absolutely none!

Sam figured that most new mothers would show some excitement when expecting a baby, but Hilda never did. He noticed how sad she looked when she was home. He would often try to talk to the baby or touch her belly, but Hilda would just pull away from him. Sam loved Hilda with his everything, but he just couldn't comprehend her cold heart.

Hilda failed to prepare herself for the baby's arrival. The nursery was utterly empty. Sam felt somewhat responsible, so he decided to decorate the room himself. First, he hired a painter to paint the walls a soft green with white trim.

The head housekeeper, Mrs. Brizzie, God bless her soul, had offered to make curtains. They turned out beautiful with green and white gingham material in a cape-cod style. She also made a matching quilt for the crib. It looked perfect.

Sam thought that there would be enough time for him to go out and buy some things for himself, but it was too late. After a few months, Hilda had gone into labor. His job also had him occupied, so he rarely got the time to focus on himself.

During the process of setting up the nursery, Mrs. Brizzie had called Meg and asked her to help. She liked Meg as she was so sweet and understanding. Colleen would come by, too.

They helped gather baby items, towels, bibs, bottles, and pins, anything that the baby would need. Colleen also passed on some of her daughter, Lillie's, things as well. Times were tight during the war, but all of them contributed to whatever they could manage.

Sam was happy to have Mrs. Brizzie around to help. She was a wonderful woman, a widow who had been forced to raise two children on her own. Both she and Mrs. Murphy, another housekeeper, were invaluable to Sam, which they proved through their loyalty and long-term services.

Sam was grateful that he had understanding people helping around the house. Only a couple of weeks after he began to set up the nursery, he had one of the biggest fights with Hilda, which left him torn and worried.

Sam arrived home bone-tired and had stumbled across Hilda sitting in the parlor. The phone was glued to her ear.

She was laughing. It was music to Sam's ears. It had been so long since he had heard Hilda laugh. Not once during her pregnancy had she even smiled, let alone laugh.

Sam stood outside the parlor door, hoping to hear her chuckle or giggle some more. Instead, he heard Hilda mocking him.

"Oh, and do you know what Sam said when I came home yesterday after shopping? He said, 'Don't worry love, we'll go shopping for the baby just as soon as I can make a little time.'" She laughed.

"Hah! Like I ever wanted to shop for the baby..." she snickered.

Sam snapped after hearing her hurtful words. He marched into the room with rage consuming every fiber in his body. He then ripped the phone cord out of the wall. Sam was usually calm and composed. He had never done anything like this before, so Hilda was completely taken by surprise.

"Sam Granger! What in the world is wrong with you?" She shouted. She stood up as Sam threw the phone cord aside. His chest was heaving with anger. He could hardly catch his breath. Hilda should have been afraid to see him this angry, but her anger defied logic.

"What are you talking about, Hilda?" He shouted, his voice echoed around the empty parlor.

"You think I'm a fool?" He again shouted at her.

"Yes, you are! The biggest fool in this world! A Dummkopf!"

"Hilda!" He yelled.

"Don't shout at me! Do you hear me? Don't think you can shout at me just because I'm carrying your baby. This baby changes everything. There is no more of 'us!' Don't you get it? I never wanted anything to get between us. This baby is doing exactly that, and it's not even born yet," Hilda yelled back.

Sam stepped closer to her. She tried to move back, but he held her by the elbows. Everything was starting to make sense to him now. The crying, sadness, and angry outbursts were not only for mourning the body she was losing, but the child she was bringing into the world. Sam found this to be selfish.

She avoided his eyes, trying not to notice the rage that was brewing in his once loving eyes. For once, she was stunned into silence as Sam grabbed her face. His grip was firm but not enough to hurt her. He brushed his nose against her.

"Everything will change, Hilda. Starting from now, things will change," he said. He pinched her lips close together like a fish and pushed her back on the bed. Hilda gritted her teeth as she stared up at Sam and saw a monster looking back. Her loving husband was gone.

He shouted, "You are my wife! We took vows together to love and respect each other! Till death do us part, remember? Do you remember that, Hilda?"

It had been so long since he called her by her real name. He always called her Hildie in endearment, but that affection was gone now. He no longer felt that way about her, at least for now. He looked desperate and close to tears, but Hilda's cold expressions didn't budge. It seemed all Hilda could think about was the anger brewing inside her. Meanwhile, Sam was seething inside as well.

Sam had gotten a telegram earlier that Zeke was missing in action following the battle of Anzio in Italy. His nerves were on edge for a week now. He had only received one letter from Zeke since his enlistment. Zeke was not allowed to tell him where he was. Sam kept that one letter in his billfold. He took it out and read it whenever he missed his brother.

It always brought him comfort. It read:

Dear Brother,

I know you, so I'm not going to say 'don't worry' because you will worry about me anyway. But don't worry ha-ha. We are eating well and also getting some rest. Fighting has slowed down. My boots hurt my feet from all the walking. I'm glad to be able to have some quiet time. I have some good buddies here. We have this Mexican cook Jorge who thinks he's great at cooking, but I hope to never eat spam and eggs again for as long as I live. I would love to get a decent cup of blackstrap. The stuff they give out here is like tar. Even your coffee is better, ha-ha.

Everyone has a nickname here that I find to be funny. Luka is 'The Singer.' He sings everywhere without even reading the atmosphere. It would be nice if he could actually sing, though. Billy is 'The Banker.' He is always counting every penny that he sends home so that he can buy his mama a car. Benny is 'Romeo.' That man can't stay away from a mirror! Then, there's Jason, and he's from Tarrytown. Go figure! We call him 'Cowboy' because he knows a lot about farming.

I'll tell ya mine when I get home. All jokes aside, these boys are the best. The guys all have photographs of their girls pinned up on their bags. I was wondering if Hilda would send me one of hers. I'm only kidding, brother! I'm so happy for you, too. Seriously, she doesn't know that she has the greatest husband ever. I know as your brother that you are a diligent man. I don't need to remind you of this. You're much more responsible and caring than me, but take care of her. I know she loves you.

Right now, I can't say where I am, nor do I know when you will get my letters. We barely get the time to write here, but don't worry. I'm a Granger! We're all as tough as Dad! I'll be home before you know it. I love you, Sam. A kiss for my sister-in-law, too.

Always, Z.

Sam cried every time he finished reading that letter. He had been so worried, and now Zeke was missing. "It should be me," he thought to himself on multiple occasions. He drove home, hoping to see his wife to comfort himself, but he found her degrading him. It was more than he could take.

"This baby…" Hilda started, but the terrifying look on Sam's face scared Hilda for the first time. Sam cut her off,

"You mean our baby, Hilda. That is our child that you are carrying in there."

Hilda seemed aggravated by Sam's comment, and it showed. "You imply that I wanted a baby. I didn't!" She got off the bed and began to walk away. But Sam was not going to let her get away so easily. "What's wrong with you?" He yelled at her. He could not believe Hilda was even saying this. He never thought that a mother wouldn't love her own baby.

"You're asking...what's wrong with me?" Hilda looked stunned.

She stepped toward him, "What's wrong with me? No, Sam, there is nothing wrong with me. Everything is wrong with you! Don't you see it? I loved us, and by us, I mean you and me. I loved it when I was the only one on your mind, but now all you think about is this baby. I was your baby. Now, you want to love this...this."

She held her bulging stomach with a hate-filled look on her face. "This baby is taking you away from me." She choked the words out. She knew that Sam would dote over the baby once it was born. All of that attention once belonged to her! Sam figured she believed that she now meant less to him.

There was a maniacal look in her eyes. It scared Sam. He had never seen this side of Hilda. He was scared of what Hilda might do to this baby if he couldn't stop her. If his love was not enough to convince her, he would have to scare her into doing the right thing. He knew just the right way to do so.

"If you don't act like a mother and a wife from this moment on, I won't be giving you any money anymore! That's all that you care about anyways," Sam said and threw the telegram at her.

Hilda paused, turned around, and glowered at him. Sam was unmoved by it. He pushed past her and slammed the door behind him. All the while, Hilda found herself wishing that she could understand why she felt such disdain for the baby. She felt helpless. She knew that he was not wrong.

It wasn't about the money, at least up until now. She couldn't bring herself to do anything and only wasted her time crying, getting angry, and falling victim to feelings of despair. This overwhelming despair convinced her that the future was bleak. She read the telegram, and her heart sunk.

"Zeke, oh no….."

Hilda liked Zeke. He was the closest she ever got to having a real sibling.

Sam didn't want to spend even a minute with his wife, so he left the house immediately. He went into town and spent the night at a local motel. It was not like him to stay out all night while his wife stayed at home, but he didn't care at the moment. He was too angry at Hilda and was scared that he might act on his anger. He was also worried about Zeke, so he didn't want to take out his frustration on Hilda.

As those dark thoughts invaded Sam's mind, he found it impossible to drift off to sleep. He relived the argument that had taken place over and over again while tossing and turning in the hard mattress of the motel.

That night, Sam prayed for the first time in years, "Dear God, please, I'm not much of a religious man, but I beg you to calm my anger. Please, God, spare my brother. Show me what to do."

He cried to himself. He watched the sunrise through his bedroom window with his puffy eyes. With a defeated sigh, he got up and headed home.

He wondered how he could be so cruel to her as he drove all the way back home. He considered she was right and that he was nothing but an idiot. All women get unpredictable when they're pregnant. He should have cut her some slack. He pulled into the driveway. He entered the kitchen from the rear-entry door.

He noticed Mrs. Brizzie fixing breakfast for Hilda, which she did each morning. She always prepared two eggs poached in milk placed over toast and had a fresh pot of coffee on the stove.

"Good morning, Mr. Granger Sir, would you like to have breakfast?" she said with a kind smile.

Mrs. Brizzie was an older woman. Her white hair was always in a hairnet. She was on the plump side, but that appealed to her sweet demeanor. She was also a great cook and kept the kitchen spotless. It was a shame that a woman like her was widowed. She had lost her husband in the first war in 1918. Sam remembered her husband Antonio, who had once worked as a butcher in his father's meat store. He was only a kid back then, but the memories were vivid.

Antonio had joined the army in 1917 and was killed in France during the awful trench warfare that engulfed much of the fighting. He left a wife and two daughters behind. The daughters had grown into two fine women. Mrs. Brizzie had seen to that. She always expressed her gratitude for having an employer like Samuel Granger. There were not a lot of people who would employ a 60-year-old widow.

Sam never made her feel as if her employment was an act of charity. She earned her keep in the house because she was an excellent cook and managed everything with utter perfection. She was a Godly woman, too. She minded her business, even when Sam knew she had a few things to say to him. She was always sensitive enough to know when to approach a certain topic or just let it be.

When it came to Hilda, whatever she said was always out of the concern and with extreme discretion.

"Mrs. Murphy already cleaned your study if you'd like to have breakfast in there." she offered.

Mrs. Murphy was the other housekeeper who was less skilled at keeping her opinions to herself. Younger than Mrs. Brizzie, she was a retired schoolteacher who had never married nor had any children of her own. She absolutely despised Germans. She did not take too kindly to Hilda and had openly told Sam that Hilda needed a good kick in the butt.

In Sam's eyes, her opinionated hatred of all things German was harmless. She did cross the line at times, but she was opinionated with everyone just the same. So, Sam didn't fret over it. He enjoyed her spark for life. She had this unique sweetness to her and often joked around. She always made him laugh. Sam tried to find a smile this time, but he could only manage a grimace.

"No, that won't be necessary, Mrs. Brizzie. Thank you," he said and walked past her, not even sure of what he was saying. His mind was occupied with his wife. He wanted to apologize to his poor, pregnant wife as quickly as possible.

He entered the bedroom and hoped to see Hilda sleeping peacefully on their king-sized bed. But to his surprise, he found her on the floor. There was a small pool of blood under her legs.

"No, no, no! Hilda!" he gasped, running straight toward her. He knelt on the floor and tried to pick up her head. He lightly slapped her face a few times and sprinkled water, but her eyes didn't open.

"Wake up!" he yelled. He tried everything, but she was not responding.

"Get help!" He yelled at the top of his lungs. Mrs. Brizzie didn't waste another second as she ran down the stairs. She grabbed the phone, only to find that the cord had been ripped from the wall.

Sam feared the worst while he cried and tried to wake his wife. "Oh, what have I done? I'm so sorry, Hildie...oh please, darling. Please, stay with me," he pleaded. Despair was written all over his face.

"Get me my keys!" he screamed. Mrs. Brizzie ran upstairs with a frantic look on her face.

"The phone, sir! It's not working. Mrs. Murphy has run over to the neighbor's home to call an ambulance," she informed. She knelt down and picked up Hilda's hand, checking for a pulse. She felt a strong pulse, so she sighed in relief. She applied a cold cloth to Hilda's head and slapped her, a bit harshly.

Mrs. Brizzie looked up at Sam. Breathing deeply, she

said, "Now, listen carefully, I've had babies myself, so there is nothing to panic here. Losing a little blood is normal when the water breaks. Try not to push. Wait for the ambulance to arrive. Your baby is on the way, Hilda."

Mrs. Brizzie tried to calm Hilda down, but she noticed that Sam's presence was making it challenging for Hilda to relax. Thinking quickly, she asked Sam to get Hilda another cold rag for her head. Her tone left no doubt. It was firm as if enforcing that this was an important order to follow.

Sam quickly complied. Then, she tried to soothe the panicking Hilda. Each time Sam returned, he was sent on another errand. This was also to keep him from falling apart until the ambulance arrived.

The last thing Hilda needed was to see Sam panic. The ambulance finally arrived after what felt like forever. Two men in white uniforms came rushing through the front doors. With a stretcher in their hands, they bounded up the steps. Hilda was laid on the stretcher and placed in the back of the ambulance.

Sirens blared away as Hilda remained half alert. They made their way to Mt. Sinai Hospital. Sam drove as fast as he could just to keep up with them.

This was how they ended up at the hospital. After a series of fights and shouting at each other for hours, the time for giving birth finally came. His wife's painful screams still echoed in the waiting room.

Sam sighed to himself, trying to figure out where he found the strength to deal with those nine months Hilda was pregnant. Those terrible months finally led to this day. As much as it hurt Sam to hear his wife wince and whine in pain, he was still happy to hear that she was well enough to curse at him.

At this point, Sam had been restlessly kicking his heels for hours in the waiting room. He couldn't bear to hear Hilda's continuous screaming. He drank cup after cup of strong black coffee, attempting to calm himself.

He had also called Eva before he left for the hospital. She had headed over to the house and was waiting with Mrs. Brizzie and Mrs. Murphy. Sam had tried to convince her to come, but she politely declined his offer. She told him babies were just not her thing, so she had no idea how to help a new mother. She also didn't think of herself as a role model, nor did she aspire to be one. Yet, the thought of becoming a new aunt was growing on her.

***

Eva wished that she could call her sister in Germany, but the war made that impossible. She would have loved to tell them that Hilda was doing fine and that she was about to have a baby. They would be so excited to become an Oma (Grandmother) and Opa (grandfather) for the first time. She was sure they would have loved to be there for Hilda's wedding. And now she was having a baby!

However, no one had heard from either of them for a long time now. Eva feared that they might be numbered with the growing war victims.

Only time would tell. After Eva had hung up with Sam, she quickly drove over to their home with a gift neatly wrapped in light purple paper and long ribbons. She arrived at the house, finding Mrs. Brizzie and Mrs. Murphy cleaning the bathroom floor where Hilda had fallen. Eva politely offered to help, but she was waved off by the two ladies who worked feverishly to clean up as quickly as possible.

Eva was looking forward to seeing the nursery. Her excitement turned to gloom upon viewing the somewhat empty green room. Despite Sam seeming excited to become a father, the condition of the room suggested something else. There was no furniture or decorations.

There was nothing except a small box with a quilt and some nice curtains on the wall. Colleen and Meg had also collected a few items but not much. Eva knew that Hilda didn't want a baby. Hilda had said that much to her on numerous occasions, but she never realized that her niece could be so selfish as to not even buy a crib for her baby.

Eva told the ladies that she was heading out for a while and would be back soon. She went to the baby's section at the Haversmith's and immediately placed an order for a crib and some nursery furniture. She requested swift delivery to the house.

She had a small amount of money saved with the intention of eventually paying her sister back the money she had borrowed from her. It had always been Eva's intention to bring Yusef and Britta to America. With the ruthless war reaching its peak and the total silence from their side, the situation was looking bleak.

The allies had landed in France, and the push toward Germany was progressing rapidly. Allied bombers were striking Germany from all sides now. The Russian forces were relentless, seeking revenge for the ferocity and brutality that the German forces had inflicted on their home soil.

This conflict was coming to a climax. Eva feared for Yusef and Britta. How could they survive what was happening? The American dream seemed only a dream.

As Eva came home, she counted the money she had left. The more she stared at the notes, the more she remembered her sister suffering in Germany. She shook her head to purge the thought. Today was a vital day.

Eva informed the ladies about what she had done. They were both thrilled and offered to help set up the nursery with her. The ladies got to work. They sewed, knitted, and cleaned. They were excitedly preparing the nursery for the baby's arrival.

They drank tea together and told stories as they awaited the furniture's arrival. Finally, the Howland truck pulled up to the house. They unloaded the crib first. It was white with a green canopy. It perfectly matched the curtains and quilt that Mrs. Brizzie had made. They put a matching white dresser against the far wall with the changing table nearby.

Next, they loaded the dresser with diapers and pins, burp cloths, white tee shirts, booties in all colors, bonnets for a girl, and a cap for a boy. They were still unsure of the baby's gender. Eva stood by the nursery door. She looked at the crib, the bookshelf with all types of children's books, the dresser, and the changing table. She smiled softly. In only a couple of hours, the gloomy, empty room looked colorful and vibrant.

She tried to picture Hilda taking care of her baby in this room. Suddenly, it all hit her with full force. She began to weep. She was going to be an aunt. A great aunt! Never in her life had she felt such emotion as she did now. Hilda would be a mother soon, whether she wanted to be or not. She glanced around the newly-decorated room once again and blinked away her tears. Eva hoped that motherhood would make Hilda a more responsible person.

Eva always shrugged off Hilda's constant complaining. She believed that once the baby arrived, Hilda's maternal instincts would kick in.

However, Eva would soon be proven wrong.

***

Adal Sarah Granger came into the world on August 25, 1944. She was a beautiful, healthy baby, weighing 6lb 3oz. She had a full head of reddish-brown hair that stood up in every direction. Unlike other babies, Adal didn't come out screeching. She seemed to be in a sweet slumber, only crying when the doctor slapped her little bottom to check her lungs. All the nurses cooed over her. As the doctor brought her toward her mother, Hilda turned away.

"I don't want to hold her," she refused. She didn't even want to look at the baby, much to everyone's shock. The nurses in the room looked at Hilda in frustration before cleaning Adal up. "Another mom with the baby blues," they whispered amongst themselves. Nurse Helen said, "Shh, she will hear you, and besides, I recently read about some mothers having severe breakdowns during this time. There's a new study on it."

"Barbaric!" They agreed.

Just then, one of the nurses ran down the hall in total hysteria. "What's wrong with her," one nurse asked the other.

"Her son was just drafted," she answered.

"Oh dear, not another one."

Nurse Helen brought Adal to her father, not sure what to expect. To her surprise, he was thrilled to meet his daughter. Sam cried as he rocked her in his arms. He just didn't want to put her down. He instantly fell in love with his baby daughter. He took out a photograph from his billfold of his brother. "This is Uncle Zeke. He's the best uncle ever, and he is coming home soon to meet you. I just know that you both will be the best of friends," he said.

He held her as if he had been a father before. He was a natural. The nurses were satisfied to see that at least one of the parents was happy to see the child.

The nurses took her away to rest. Adal made no noises in her room. She was the only quiet baby in the nursery. Sam spent hours standing by the window, staring at his daughter. He couldn't wait to hold his baby again. He would do anything only to see her open her eyes.

As it turned out, Adal's birthday would long be remembered. On August 25, 1944, France was liberated.

Half of the world was rejoicing, while Germany had weakened and was going to be defeated.

After leaving the hospital, Sam rushed to the theater and watched the newsreels just so he could catch a glimpse of Zeke. There was news of survivors and the dead. It was all terrible! From that point on, when he was not with Adal or working, he was glued to the radio.

Eva arrived the next day to see Adal. She also fell in love at first sight. The moment Eva held Adal in her arms, something inside her awoke. She wished for the first time in her life for a baby of her own.

Eva had never wanted to be a mother, but holding Adal in her arms seemed to stir some sort of maternal instinct within her. She couldn't stop smiling. She thought of Britta and Yosef at that moment. They may never know this little girl.

In the following months, Hilda hardly held Adal. She certainly had not developed any maternal instinct. As soon as she arrived back home, she immediately hired a nurse to take care of the baby. Mrs. Wheeler was a live-in nurse. She was a middle-aged woman in her mid-forties. Her love for babies was enough to satisfy Sam, and he hired her. Her room was located right next to Adal's so that if Adal cried in the middle of the night, she could quickly come and tend to her.

Mrs. Wheeler had no children of her own. Her husband had also been killed in the war. She was forced to work to support herself, just like Mrs. Brizzie and Mrs. Murphy.

Mrs. Wheeler adored Adal. She believed that all children were a blessing. She treated Adal with the same tenderness that she had provided to the other children that she had raised and cared for over the years. But Adal's circumstances were different! Mrs. Wheeler noted as time passed that Adal really didn't have a mother.

Hilda rarely set foot in the nursery. She had given Mrs. Wheeler express instructions that she should not be disturbed, either day or night, unless there was an emergency. Even when Hilda had mentioned this, it was apparent from her rigid expressions that she didn't want to be associated with Adal in any way.

Mrs. Wheeler had seen many mothers over the years, but none of them came close to Hilda. "Someone needs to set that woman straight!" She muttered as she passed Mrs.

Murphy in the hallway after meeting Hilda in the parlor. Mrs. Murphy heard and chuckled, "I agree. That woman needs a good kick in the arse."

Leaning close, she whispered, "This is nothing. You should have seen her when she was actually pregnant. Mrs. Granger was a walking mummy."

Mrs. Wheeler clicked her tongue, rudely, "She doesn't deserve to be a mother. She's not even human. What kind of mother doesn't even spend a single moment with her newborn child?"

She stopped outside the nursery room. She was glad that at least one of them cared about their baby as she stared at Sam holding Adal. He was rocking and cooing to her as any happy father would. Sam couldn't keep away from Adal. He wanted nothing more than to spend every waking moment with her. Adal was part of Hilda and him, and though she was not motherly, he still loved her.

Sam loved his daughter with all his heart. He read to her every night and told her stories of growing up with Grampa Charlie and Grandma Annabelle. She pretty much knew everything about Uncle Zeke.

Sam never missed a day talking about his brother to her. He taught her to pray for him to return safely. He even sang her songs, and when he could, he took her for walks in the park. They bonded nicely.

Adal was growing up well. She was beautiful in his eyes. She had Hilda's brown eyes that shone like marbles in the sunlight. He would spend every possible moment with her, not wanting to miss anything.

Hilda, on the other hand, just spent her time shopping. She made sure that she wore the best clothes, went to cinemas to stay entertained, and frequented numerous parties with her friends Meg and Colleen. Colleen, now a widow with 3-year-old Lily, went back home and lived on the farm that she despised. She had no choice.

She was unable to support herself and her daughter after her husband's death. She had to go back and live with her family. Colleen had no issue going into the city for a night or two of fun as she hated home. Hilda also joined the Garden Club summer party committee. She seemed to make time for anything except Adal. Sam was not being fooled. Hilda saw how Sam treated Adal.

Whenever she had dinner with Sam, he would place Adal on his lap, feed her first, and then eat his dinner. After dinner, he would change Adal despite Mrs. Wheeler's insisting that it was her job. He would also put her to sleep.

Sam bought Adal everything. He got her toys, clothes, and shoes of the best quality. He denied Hilda nothing, but Hilda was well aware that she was no longer number one in Sam's life. She could not stand it. She was jealous of the attention that Adal was given. When Hilda talked to Sam, he would include Adal in the conversation at some point.

"Adal tried to walk! You should have seen the way she wobbled on her feet, Hildie," Sam said one night before they were about to go to sleep. Hilda only rolled her eyes. She took off her earrings to get ready for bed.

Sam persisted, "I can't believe she's growing up so fast. Do you think we should buy her that doll we saw today on the way home from dinner? I hope Adal didn't notice that we were gone."

Hilda only sighed in irritation. "Can you stop it already?" She snapped.

Sam was in the middle of taking his shoes off. He paused after hearing Hilda's harsh tone. "You sound as if I'm talking about another woman instead of our own daughter." Sam snapped back as a matter of fact.

Hilda got under the covers quickly, "Honestly, at this point, I would rather hear you talk about another woman. At least, then, I would understand why...." she said, then paused. No, she would hate it even more if Sam did talk about other women. She mimicked Sam's voice poorly. The anger she had been feeling for the past year seemed to reach its peak.

"I'm tired," she changed the topic. Sam had heard her and was bewildered. He growled, "Well, if you spent more time with her, you would get to know her. You would really know how precious our little girl is."

"There you go again!" She exclaimed and sat up on the bed with an angry scowl on her face. "Why do you have to blame me for everything?"

"Because you're frivolously draining our bank account, and you are a terrible excuse for a mother! This is not helping our family life."

"Why do you care about money? I'm not the only one spending it! You keep spending on Adal like its Christmas every other day!" she screamed.

Sam retorted, "She's our daughter, Hilda! We're her parents. We're supposed to make sure she gets everything she needs. Yes, I spend more than I should, but did I ever deprive you of the same?"

Hilda scoffed at him.

"Well, if you stopped spending so much on her, we wouldn't have a problem with money in the first place," she replied.

Sam moved back.

She added, "We don't have a money problem, but you are not financially wise. If we never had her…"

Hilda stopped herself from speaking further, knowing how horrible she sounded to her husband. She was not sure if she loved her child or not. She felt detached from Adal. She didn't hate Adal per se, but there was just no maternal instinct in her, even if she tried to force it out of herself. She honestly didn't understand it herself. She often wondered why she couldn't bond with her.

"You really are..." he trailed off. "If you had an ounce of motherly love inside your heart, you would have never said that. Let me tell you one more time, Hilda. If you don't start showing some attention to Adal, I'll cut you off from everything I own," Sam said calmly and walked out of the room.

Even though he really didn't mean it, it felt good to say that to her. Hilda brewed in her anger in the bedroom. After that night, Sam never brought up her lack of maternal instincts again. He was furious at her, but he feared that there was something wrong with his wife. He didn't want to trigger a mental breakdown.

They pretended to tolerate each other over the next two years. Their lives were the same, but this time, without any fights or arguments. They tried to ignore each other's flaws every day as Sam took care of Adal, while Hilda continued to ignore her daughter.

The war ended on September 2, 1945. It was a catastrophic ending to a war that went on for six years. Some soldiers came home, but many did not. There was no word from Zeke. Germany had been conquered, and Japan had been occupied. Eva and Hilda never heard from Yusef and

Britta again. Like so many other post-war families, they had no answers. Hilda missed her father the most. She was close to her mother, but her father gave her all his attention. She prayed to a God that she was not so sure she believed in. The war had taken a heavy toll on all sides.

Sam's business's continued to prosper. The post-war economy was booming. Financially, things had never been better for Sam. His life at home was quite different, though. Months had passed since the end of the war, and he still had no word from Zeke. He feared the worst but prayed for the best.

Sam gave a lot to soldiers and their families. He tried his best to land them jobs, give them money and food, anything in his power. He visited them in hospitals and bought toys for their children during Christmas. He would take Adal with him to teach her about the honor of giving. He overcompensated for his guilt of not being able to fight in the war himself and his missing brother.

Sam was a good man, and Hilda saw this even more now. She wanted his love in return. The only way to do so was through bonding with Adal. He would love it if Hilda gave their daughter attention. She did try to bond with her daughter, but there just wasn't anything there. She had no maternal instinct at all.

Hilda pretended to be a mother to Adal to at least remain attached to Sam's wallet if she couldn't be in his heart. If she couldn't be Sam's alone, at least she would have his money. Hilda was ready to do anything to have Sam's money. Would she even sell her soul?

"Till death do us part." She remembered her vows. Till death do us part made sense.

Chapter 5
Tim

Timothy Kelly was content with the way things were going with his life. Farming had always been a part of his identity. He was a simple man who earned a modest living from the Red Top farm that he owned. The farm had been passed down to him when his grandfather had passed away several years ago.

For Tim, gaining the farm was exciting, but losing his grandfather was bittersweet. He had endured enough losses in his short life. Losing a loved one weighed heavily on Tim.

He had lost both of his parents at an early age. He was raised by his grandfather, and so was his older brother, Jason, and sister, Colleen. Tim's older brother, Jason Kelly, became a marine. He was killed in the Anzio campaign in early January of 1944. His death hit Tim very hard. The suddenness of the loss left him breathless.

When Tim received the Western Union telegram, Tim's world just seemed to stop. Still, he figured he would adjust as quickly as he had when his grandfather had died a few years earlier.

Now that he thought about it, he realized that he had watched his grandfather deteriorate slowly over the years. This allowed Tim time to adjust to his eventual passing gradually. He reminisced about how strong his grandfather was and how his sickness reduced him to being exhausted by only going from one room to another. Once energetic and able to work sunup to sundown, he was eventually bedridden until his death. The process saddened Tim greatly.

However, Jason's death was the first sudden loss in Tim's life. His parents had passed away when he was only four that left Jason, Tim, and Colleen as orphans. His grandparents quickly took them all in and raised them together. They never felt as if they were orphaned. When their grandma passed away, Grandpa took over all the parenting responsibilities.

Perhaps, that was why the sudden loss of Jason hit Tim as hard as it did. The profound grief made Tim feel utterly vulnerable. He decided that he had to be strong for his sister Colleen who had recently lost her husband in the war, as well. The war had taken so many husbands, fathers, and brothers. It seemed like every day, someone they knew received a dreaded telegram.

Colleen's husband, John Logan, died in the early days of the Normandy invasion. She was left with their infant daughter and barely managed to scrape by. Supporting herself as a young mother became quite challenging.

Tim knew the consequences of joining the army, but he would have given anything to serve his country. He had suffered a tractor accident when he was 13. His arm had been fractured in several places.

The army had deemed him incapable of service. Like every other patriotic American, Tim still wanted to do his part. Farming allowed him the opportunity to help feed the hungry troops that fought overseas and pass on extra crops to the needy families in the area.

When Jason left for the war, Tim promised his older brother that he would watch over the family. He considered it an honor to protect his sister and grandparents. He wanted the farm to thrive, so Jason had something to come home to. He felt this way until his brother's unfortunate fate.

Colleen seemed to have a tougher time than Tim did. It was during this time that she had been notified of her husband John's death in the days immediately after the D-day invasion.

Like most patriotic Americans, John was eager to fight for his country. He realized that freedom was never free. The price had to be paid. He left behind a wife and an infant daughter at the time. Colleen had heard that he fought bravely. He indeed paid the ultimate price like thousands of others.

"Uncle Tim! Uncle Tim!" His only niece, Lily, chirped as she ran into the barn excitedly. Before Tim could look back, she had thrown her little arms around his back. She was smiling wide. Her small arms could only reach halfway around Tim's wide neck. Tim stood 6'8 tall and tipped the scales at over 250lbs.

Lily just saw him as a big, soft teddy bear. "You won't believe what happened today," Lily said. Tim made a delighted sound.

"Well, I'd love to hear about it!" he laughed as he turned his head around and looked at her with adoring eyes. His little 3-year-old niece had inherited the same bright blue eyes that he had. He also had a shock of curly red hair that he tucked under the brim of his grandfather's old hunting cap, which he wore proudly.

Tim loved his niece more than anything. He found it tough to refuse her anything. For now, she wanted to sit on his lap and help milk the cow. She excitedly relayed her 'story of the day' as Tim performed the task at hand with care. He was a professional farmer. He could multitask with even the most challenging of farming chores.

Nothing special had really happened today, but Lily was always thrilled to share her day with her uncle Tim. Tim remembered sitting on his grandfather's lap and telling stories just like Lily.

Grandpa Kelly had taken his grandchildren into his home when they had become orphans, without even blinking an eye. Tim was too young to remember what his parents even looked like. He immediately accepted Grandpa as a father figure in his life.

It took a little longer for Jason and Colleen to do the same as they were both older and more aware of the changing circumstances. So, they had a hard time acknowledging the fact that their father was gone and see this man as a replacement. After milking the cows, both of them headed back to the farmhouse. Lily trailed behind, dragging a small tin bucket that splashed warm milk all over the sides.

"Make sure that you don't spill it, Lil," he said with a grin as she happily skipped her way back to the farmhouse. This little bucket had been specially made for her tiny hands. "I won't drop any, Uncle Tim! Don't worry," she smiled at him and chattered away happily.

They both entered the house to see Colleen washing dishes at the sink. She turned around and greeted her brother with a stern expression on her face.

Tim came over to peck her on the forehead as he always did.

"Hello, you look a little tired," he said. Tim was quite used to Colleen's mood swings by now. She had always had a serious side that just didn't bother him anymore. Colleen had taken on the role of being Tim's mother when their parents had passed away. She had been there for Tim since he was as small as Lily.

"Lily-Rose Logan!" Colleen started sternly. "Uh, oh," Lily mumbled as Colleen placed her fists on her waist.

"What have I told you about playing in the barn with your good dress on? You were told to change into your barn clothes."

Colleen was taller than most women. She stood at 5'9". Unlike her daughter and brother, she had light green eyes and blonde hair. She was fair as compared to Tim, who had a darker skin tone due to working outdoor for hours. Even in winter, Tim never took a break from the farm. His hands and back were as tough as leather. The ladies found him to be attractive, though, not that Tim would ever notice.

"I was helping Uncle Tim!" Lily pouted, looking up at her mother with an adorable expression, "And we were getting some milk, mama! Look, mama, Uncle Tim was able to get so much milk," she said and held up the bucket.

Colleen sighed tiredly, "What will I ever do with these two?"

She loved how these two had bonded. Tim patted the back of Lily's head with a big, goofy smile, "It's OKAY, Colleen. I made sure she didn't chase the cows again."

He was referring to the time Lily had run around the barn and nearly stampeded the cows right out with her energy.

Colleen again sighed, "Go ahead and wash up, both of you. I'll get your supper on the table."

Colleen and Lily used to live in an apartment near the city. Colleen wanted to expose Lily to what the city life had to offer them. Colleen barely made enough to make ends meet; she still tried to manage. But soon, it all became too hard to bear, and she had to settle on the farm with her daughter.

She always wanted to make sure that Tim had a hot meal. He worked too hard just to have a sandwich for dinner. She did all of it out of love. A home-cooked meal was the least she could do. It was better than eating at Jack's Diner every day, which was precisely what he did when she didn't leave him any food.

Both Tim and Lily saluted with their right hands. They said, "Yes, ma'am," under their breaths. Colleen hid her smile at their silliness. All she could muster was, "Hurry up, now."

Tim went into the bathroom to wash up. He then changed into a fresh set of clothes. It was such a relieving moment for him as this signaled the end of another day's labor.

Tim maintained a rigorous work schedule, often beginning before dawn and not finishing until late in the evening. Today was an exception. He completed most of his work early that allowed him to enjoy some supper and perhaps a short nap before finishing woodcutting.

Tim and Lily washed up before they sat down at the dinner table. Colleen had made them spaghetti and meatballs, Lily's favorite! They whispered their graces and ate heartily.

However, Colleen just played with her food. She didn't feel like eating much these days, and Tim had noticed this. When dinner was over, Lily wanted to play with one of the new chocolate lab puppies out in the front yard. Tim was helping his sister with the dishes. They both kept a close eye on Lily through the window.

"How are you feeling these days, Colleen?" Tim asked out of concern. Colleen just shrugged. "I'm fine," she said flatly. Tim just frowned.

"I noticed that you didn't eat anything for supper."

Colleen pursed her lips and remained silent for a full minute. Tim had had enough of the silence. He spun his sister around to face him. "Are you feeling alright? Maybe, you take some rest," Tim advised. Colleen only shook her head.

"I ate before both of you came in. I'll be fine. You don't have to worry about me," she reassured.

Tim knew that Colleen was only putting up walls again. She did this whenever he would pry into her personal life. It was obvious how much Colleen had changed since losing Jason and her husband, John.

All the added responsibility caused Colleen to become more serious and struggle with bouts of anger. She distracted herself by focusing on Lily and her brother, the only family that she had left. She did her best to take care of them both.

In some ways, Tim was just like Lily. He knew how to take care of an entire farm, but he couldn't take care of himself. He didn't push the issue any further and let it be for now. "Get some rest," he said before going outside to play with Lily for a while.

Colleen sighed and placed a bowl on the kitchen windowsill. She stared at Tim's giant frame playing outside ever so gently with little Lily. She smiled. She wished that

Tim would get married, raise a family of his own, and then sell this farm. He loved children. She knew that he would do anything for Lily.

It wasn't that Colleen was tired of taking care of her brother. She just wanted to see him spend his energy on things other than this farm. It was true that he was the sole owner despite them being siblings. Grandpa Kelly had left this property in his will to Tim alone. He was the favorite grandchild. He was the one Grandpa felt could run the farm well, and all of that was evident from the very beginning.

Grandpa expected Jason and Colleen to mentor young Tim and watch over him. The fact that Grandpa would remind them both of this often didn't seem to bother them. They loved their younger brother. Still, it was tough on them as well as they were children themselves.

Colleen and Jason had fond memories of their early life in Yonkers. They were close enough to take the train to New York City. They rode horses in Central Park and shopped in many stores along 2156 5th Avenue. They remembered Christmas in that city to be the best experience of their lives. Adjusting to farm life had been challenging for them. It was quite boring. Tim was only four at the time, so his experience was different. He actually loved living on the farm with all the pigs, goats, chickens, and cows. Tim learned to take care of them all.

He had several dogs over the years, but he loved his black Labrador, Shadow, the best. He named him Shadow since he never left his side. Even when Tim attended church on Sunday, faithful Shadow waited in his pickup truck's bed.

Shadow and another lab dog, Willow-Girl, just had a litter of puppies. Lily loved to play with them. Tim was the only sibling who truly resembled his father as he had red hair. Colleen was well aware that her grandfather viewed Tim as his own son, not just a grandchild.

When Grandpa had gotten older, he would sometimes call Tim by his late father's name. Tim didn't seem to mind. He realized that Grandpa's memory was not what it used to be.

Tim was glad to be with Grandpa when he died. He lived a life of faith, attended weekly services, and didn't fear what was to come. He looked forward to seeing his beloved wife again. She would be free of pain, young, and oh... so beautiful in heaven. He passed away quietly before whispering the name 'Evelyn' into the wind.

In his will, Grandpa, surprisingly, left the entire 100-acre farm and home in Tarrytown to Tim alone. He gave both Colleen and Jason a sum of money. He specified the reason in the will. He knew Colleen and Jason would sell it out from under Tim, so he made sure that didn't happen.

Despite never wanting the farm, Colleen still felt a bit sad he thought that way. The farm managed to provide enough for Tim over the years. He was considered well off, even though he maintained a simple life. Colleen always seemed to worry about Tim's well-being. She thought of him to be gullible and easily fooled at times. She was especially leery of the church. Tim was a man of great faith like his grandfather, who became a member of the First Baptist Church of Tarrytown at the age of 18.

Tim started each day in prayer and thanksgiving instead of just attending services once or twice a week. Faithfully, Tim would sit on the front porch without minding the weather. He sat there even when it rained or snowed. There, Tim would start his day by reading God's word and praying. He never missed a Sunday service. He and Shadow could always be counted upon to reach the church in time. Tim was a generous person, always giving more than asked for.

Contrarily, Colleen thought the church was only about stealing money from fools who were willing to be cheated. She felt that Tim would give away the entire farm if the church wanted it. She struggled with an uneasy feeling deep within her.

Even at 8:30 p.m., Tim was active enough to be playing and romping around like a child. He was always so caught up in his current routine. Never once did he mention women or marriage to Colleen. But then again, she was here to carry out the duties of a big sister.

"What did he need a wife for," she thought to herself. Despite feeling somewhat betrayed by her grandfather, she still cleaned the house and cooked meals for her brother. She took good care of him. She would bring groceries, and sometimes, even help out in the garden by picking the vegetables. She would gladly continue to do this for her brother, but it just didn't sit well with her. She needed to have a good talk with him.

With that thought in mind, she decided it was time to have this discussion a few weeks later. She was preparing supper, as always. Lily was playing with some of the farm animals while Tim was chopping some hardwood.

Colleen looked at him, thinking to herself, "He's handsome, yet he doesn't bother to date."

She shook her head. Tim caught her staring at him. "What?" he said.

"Oh, nothing," Colleen replied.

Just then, Lily came inside. She grabbed her mother's skirt and buried herself in it. She was covered in mud from head to toe. Colleen could only shake her head in frustration. She had never adjusted to farm life like Tim, yet, her daughter loved it. It was so ironic! Perhaps, her dislike stemmed from the circumstances under which she had come here in the first place. She never really got over the loss of her parents. Being the second eldest in the family, she felt responsible for caring for both of her brothers.

"Let's get you washed up before we go home," Colleen said as she scooted Lily up. Tim and Colleen had coffee on the porch, but Colleen couldn't discuss the thought tugging at her. Lily was half asleep by then. So, she put her to sleep and came to the conclusion that she would have the talk some other day.

A few days later, Colleen decided that it was the right time for her to speak about the issue. "You asked me the other day what was worrying me," she began.

This got Tim's attention as he looked up from his plate with a curious stare.

"I'm just worried about you working your life away on this darn farm. Get married and sell this place. Live a little," she told him.

Tim just sighed, "It's the only thing that Grandpa left me, uh, left us. I can't just stop working on it. I love the Red Top. It's been in our family for years now. Did you know that it was named Red Top because Grandpa Kelly's grandfather had fiery red hair?"

"No, I didn't, Timmy, nor do I care," Colleen replied.

She used his nickname, knowing that this would make him perk up. Once Tim was past the age of 16, Colleen never called him by this name anymore.

"I think it's about time that you start a family of your own," she said, her tone turning serious. Colleen was thankful that she had Tim to watch Lily when she wanted to go out with her friends or had to work. Still, she couldn't stand seeing Tim like this.

She spoke softly, "Mom didn't like the farm either."

Colleen was only saying what she felt certain their mother would have said. Colleen thought if their mother was around, she would have given Timothy an earful as he was the youngest. But she was gone now. She had died a long time ago.

Tim shrugged, "I'm fine living like this, but I'll marry if I meet the right girl. You don't have to worry about me, Colleen. I'm fine either way."

He reached down to feed a piece of chicken to Shadow, who was as always by his side. "Colleen, you don't have to cook and take care of the place. I'm doing alright."

"But I do need to worry about you, Tim, don't I? I mean… you hardly ever leave this place, and when you do, it's to go over to Jack's Diner or that church. You need to socialize more and make some friends." She said with slight agitation.

"I do have friends," he told her. "There are plenty of good people that I see every Sunday! And I got ol' Shadow here."

He reached down and patted the dog's head.

"I meant, making friends outside of there," she rolled her eyes.

"You mean, in the city?" Tim said, looking displeased with the idea.

"I enjoy being surrounded by nature. All I need are my animals to live a comfortable life. Besides, the city is far too noisy for me. I prefer the sound of animals than engines roaring. I like the smell of the fields and doing God's work with my hands." He clarified.

She reprimanded him, "It's the only way that you are going to meet a nice girl, Timmy."

Tim pondered over the idea, "The right girl for me is not in the city. I'll meet her somewhere close by, but I'll think about it."

"How about you give the church a try? You won't be judging me like this anymore," he winked.

She just smiled at him, "No, thanks."

Tim was easy to please. He didn't resist as hard as Colleen had thought. He was a good man, after all, so she was sure that he would find a woman equally as good. He was tall, handsome, and muscular, and even went to church on Sundays. This shouldn't be too hard to sell. There was a high possibility she could be able to marry him off and detach him from this farm. Colleen suddenly thought of a plan.

Chapter 6
Crash

The environment at the Granger house had not improved. On the contrary, things had gone down at a rapid pace. Sam no longer asked anything of Hilda. Whatever Adal needed, Sam spoke to Mrs. Wheeler.

Adal was growing up, yet her mother was still not willing to cradle her in her arms. She was already five years old, and still playing in Mrs. Wheeler's lap, being doted upon by everyone, except, of course, her own mother.

Each member of the Granger household had evolved into a specific role for Adal. Mrs. Brizzie had the levelheaded authoritarian attitude, but her way of correcting Adal generally included a cookie or some other nice treat. Adal was smart, too. She knew that Mrs. Brizzie's corrections somehow always ended up in tickles and giggles.

Adal also grew up with Mrs. Murphy running behind her to dress her up and taking care of her. As Adal turned five, Mrs. Murphy had taken on the role of making sure Adal was ready for school. Today was no exception.

"Get back here, young lady!" She scolded Adal as she chased her around to dress her up for school. "You can't catch me!" Adal sang as she ran around in circles, still wearing her pajamas. Sam laughed while watching the commotion unfold before him. He had a great view from the breakfast table.

Adal was still running around in circles. Her giggles echoed around the room. Adal's laughter was Sam's favorite song. He could feel that his love for Adal was quite special. The fact that she didn't have her mother's love only made Sam love her more.

When Mrs. Murphy got closer to Adal with her school clothes, Adal ducked and snuck under the table. It was a regular game that they played. Sam advised Mrs. Murphy to leave the clothes on the chair, just like he did every single day. At this point, it had become a morning routine. He pulled Adal up and sat her on his lap. She locked her twinkling eyes with him. He coaxed her into eating breakfast.

"You like pancakes, don't you?" He said in a loving tone.

"Yes!" She clapped her hands. She took a fork and stuck it into the pancakes, getting a small piece and happily munching on it. "Your bite, daddy," she said and fed her father a forkful.

Sam played with Adal's soft brown hair as she ate her breakfast. Adal was fairly well behaved. In fact, she was such a sweet little girl. Her eyes were as bright as her smile. She even had Hilda's deep dimples.

That only invoked more of Sam's affection for Adal. To Sam, Adal resembled a little doll with her reddish-brown hair, fair skin, soft brown eyes, and dark lashes. Sam loved it when Adal wore a bow in her hair with her colorful, little dresses. She was the perfect daughter for him.

Sam always found himself trying to compensate for all the love that Adal didn't receive from her mother. She was still too young to understand anything that was happening around her. Her life seemed normal, as she was only a child. There were times when Adal would ask, "Why doesn't mommy play with me?"

Sam realized that she would soon start to understand the environment in her house. She would figure out the reason why her mother never wanted even to glance her way. The thought of that day pained him deeply. Sam would reassure with, "Mommy just isn't feeling well today, honey."

A little tickle was enough to distract Adal for now. But for how long would he continue distracting her? Luckily, Mrs. Brizzie, Mrs. Murphy, and Mrs. Wheeler were the three mother figures at home for Adal. They loved her as if she were their own child.

A regular day in the house started off with Sam dressing up and feeding Adal her breakfast, getting her ready for school, and dropping her off before heading to his office. This routine gave the ladies the opportunity to catch up on some of the housekeeping chores. While all of this would be going on, Hilda would be fast asleep.

She would wake at about 11 p.m. and head out to meet with either Meg or Colleen. She wore expensive dresses, heels and always had a matching purse. Her makeup would be perfect. She would stay out all day and not return home until late in the evening.

At that point, Adal would be fast asleep. They were wholly disconnected from each other. She would do the most to avoid her daughter at all costs. The sight of this fiasco would break Sam's heart. There was a time when it appeared that Hilda was at least trying to enjoy her daughter's company, but that was short-lived. She would only allow herself to get a little close. Then, she would just shut down and pull away.

Seeing all of this, Sam's anger would almost get the best of him. He came close to striking her several times. The only thing that had stopped Sam from committing this terrible sin was that he knew this was not his true personality. He could never hurt Hilda or anyone for that matter.

Sam couldn't comprehend just who Hilda was now. She was sad and distant one day but angry and belligerent on another. She could still be sweet but only on the rarest of occasions. Her mood swings were impossible to read for Sam.

He remembered nights where she would just stare out of the window for hours. Then she would be fast asleep throughout the day. Why couldn't he figure her out? He still loved her, so he wanted to help her. Sadly, they both wanted each other. He could tell that from her eyes. One night, Sam went into the bedroom just after Mrs. Wheeler had put Adal down for bed. He slowly undid his tie. He watched Hilda change out of her dress from the corner of his eye. She was still so beautiful. He ached for her. It had been such a long time since they had made love. Hilda had grown very conscious about her body after giving birth. Her stretch marks embarrassed her, even though Sam assured her that she was still gorgeous to him. It was pure torture for Sam to see her in a white bodice, hugging all her curves so sweetly.

He approached her from behind and hugged her. She turned her head toward him. Sam placed a gentle kiss on her lips, and for once, Hilda kissed him back. She felt her heart skip a beat. "I-I can't," she stammered, pulling away from him.

Sam could not help but feel a little hopeful. He was not going to force himself upon his wife, so he retreated. "It's alright, Hildie," Sam responded. He went toward his closet to pick out a fresh pair of clothes.

Hilda sat on the edge of the bed with tears in her eyes. She wept, "I want to, Sam. I do miss your touch as much as you miss mine. But I can't do this when I know that I might get pregnant again. I can't bear the thought of going through that pain again."

Sam only looked at Hilda. His hands paused from unbuttoning his shirt. She stared back at him with glistening eyes. He wondered just what was wrong with his wife. Hilda had never been like this. He thought that her condition would get better with time. Now, he was unsure of that. "Do you hate being a mother that much?" Sam asked her. Anger welled up within him, and he was unable to contain the words.

Hilda looked at him and said, "It's not that Sam. I don't know what it is. I guess that I just can't be what you want in a wife and a mother."

He still felt angry. Avoiding her gaze, he stared at the ceiling as he struggled to control himself. He could feel himself going crazy.

"Why are you like this? Oh my God, Hilda. It's been five years, and you still can't bring yourself to accept our daughter!?" He shouted in utter frustration. Hilda just glared at Sam.

"You will never understand my anguish, Sam! How could a man know about what we go through? You were not the one who felt as if something was tearing you up from the inside out! Adal took the best part of my life and my marriage! My youth and even the love of my life are all hers! Do you think any woman can accept that?" She yelled out.

She held her head in her hands, "I don't understand this myself. I've tried. You know that I tried, but I can't stop this overwhelming fear of being her mother take over me. Why do I not want her? Mama was a great mother. I could never do all that she did for me, but I want to…I just can't!"

"Can't or won't?" Sam yelled back at her. Hilda was taken back at his comment. He realized this was more than he could deal with. She was mentally ill and needed professional help.

"What do you mean? I love Adal. I know that. You can't even understand me!" She screamed at him. Sam only shook his head before he asked again, "Answer me! Can't or won't?"

Hilda was now getting angry, noticing that Sam would not hear what she was trying to say. She responded, "Won't!"

This made Sam grab his coat in a fury and slam the door on his way out. Hilda sat frozen in place, partly out of fear from what she had said and partly out of anger. She pulled her night robe close to her body as she shook her head. "I'm not the crazy one," she mumbled under her breath. Just then, she heard a knock on the door.

"Who is it?" she shouted angrily.

The door creaked open, enough to reveal Mrs. Brizzie standing in the doorway with a concerned look on her face. "Is everything alright, Mrs. Granger? Mr. Granger ran out of the house in such a hurry," she asked. Hilda glared at her, "Yes, I'm fine. Everything is just grand."

A look of concern furrowed Mrs. Brizzie's brow, but she refrained herself from talking back. She only passed Hilda a curt nod before closing the bedroom door. Hilda heaved with anger before letting out a frustrated scream. She got up and ran a hand through her hair, glaring at her reflection in the mirror. All she could see was the ghost of her past self. She looked so miserable.

"What's happening to me?" She whispered to herself.

***

The winter's night air nipped at Sam's cheek as he made his way toward the car. He got in the vehicle, slamming the door shut. He was so furious that he couldn't care less about the icy roads. He wasn't letting his rational side win the argument. For the second time in his life, he almost regretted marrying Hilda. But he knew one thing now; she was ill. Something had taken over his sweet Hildie's mind.

He was confused. His head was spinning from negative thoughts, anger, and the overwhelming grief for what she once meant to him. He never thought that his Hildie could actually be such a vicious and cunning woman. He had a gnawing feeling that Hilda had only married him for the money.

Things were supposed to get better when you had a child. The love for this German girl had blinded him. He imagined his life to be quite different if he had a loving wife who greeted him each night. They would raise their sweet child together…a happy family.

He wished that Adal would never see a sad day, but her mother was making that dream impossible. Sam knew that he was a good father. He made sure that Adal was well taken care of. Whether it was being home for dinner or just getting her ready for bed, he was there for his daughter. He enjoyed singing her lullabies; it was undeniably the favorite time of his day. Sam knew he could call himself a good father, but what about being a good husband? This was a more complicated question. He felt guilty about not helping Hilda with her inner struggles. She was fighting those demons that wished their daughter had never been born. He spent all these years with her, yet he didn't know what thoughts pulsed through Hilda's pretty little mind.

Overcome with grief, Sam cried out. "Lord! Please, please, save Hilda from this misery. Help her find a way to be a good mother. I know you can fix her. Please!" He begged God through his tears while the car slid down the icy mountain road.

He could feel his heart just crumbling from within him. As if the night couldn't get any darker, snow began to fall. Sam turned on the wipers. He glanced in the rearview mirror. He hadn't driven that far. He could see his house, but it was slowly fading from view. The car was sliding on the icy road topped with a fresh layer of snow.

He stepped on the brakes, but it wouldn't stop. The car sped up on its own. He saw the big maple tree in front of him. It was the beautiful maple tree at the bottom of the hill that they sat by and read to each other. It brought back such loving memories that he couldn't stop staring at it.

***

Hilda was heartbroken as she gazed out the front window. She could still see the rear lights on Sam's car as he drove away. She watched him head down the steep hill. The view from the windows was clear and wide enough to display the gorgeous maple tree close to the house. The car began to slide sideways then do a full circle before slamming head-on into the same tree. Hilda screamed out loud.

She ran down the stairs, barefoot, screaming, and crying. She passed Mrs. Murphy, who was in the dining room. "Ma'am! Where are you going? Your shoes..." Mrs. Murphy yelled out.

Hilda turned to put her slippers on and ran out of the house, screeching, "What have I done?"

She ran down the ice-covered hill in nothing but her night robe and slippers. "Nein, nein, nein!" Her anguish was evident in her voice. The howling wind brushed against her face. She hardly felt it because the coldness had enveloped her body. Her sanity left her as she approached the wreck.

"Sam!! Sam!!" she screamed wildly. She reached the car

and couldn't believe her eyes. The car had struck the huge maple tree with such force that it had literally wrapped itself around it. Tiptoeing through the shattered glass on the road, Hilda called to Sam. She knelt down to see Sam trapped behind the steering wheel. The car seemed to be folded around him. She tried to pull the door open but was unable to. She looked for anything that she could use to pry the door open. There was blood all over the steering wheel.

"Hildie," Sam called out to her weakly. Hilda felt helpless while using up all her strength to pull Sam out from the wreck. "I love you," he managed to say. She could only hush him and bellow for help.

Mrs. Murphy heard all the commotion and called the police immediately. After that, she ran down the long hill with a blanket, coat, and shoes for Hilda. She had the presence of mind to grab a crowbar out of the garage, as well.

"I called for help," she yelled, running down the hill.

"Save your energy, Sam. Help is on the way; you're going to be fine," Hilda reassured him.

Sam shook his head. "You're going to be fine, Meine Liebe," she comforted. She ran her hand over his bleeding head. She and Mrs. Murphy tugged at the door together and were able to pry it open. They pulled Sam out and wrapped him in a blanket. There was blood dripping from his head, and his face was covered in cuts and bruises.

"I love you, Hildie. I am so sorry for everything…I love you…" Sam managed to say. His voice was fading. He slowly closed his eyes as if he had drifted to sleep. He closed his eyes so gently it seemed that no one would be able to wake him now.

"No, No, No!" Hilda cried hysterically. "No, don't you dare leave me!"

A small crowd had gathered by the wreck. People shook their heads in agony at the poor scene. "Don't you dare leave me alone, Sam Granger! I love you, Sam. I do. I love you. I swear, I do! Please don't leave me. I'm so sorry, Sam, I love-" She kept repeating the same words over and over again until the police came.

One of the officers had to pull her away. She was in a state of shock. Her hands shook with such intensity that she was scared they would fall off. They were coated with Sam's blood. She no longer knew where she was. Her eyes were drooping from the mental and physical exhaustion after witnessing this grisly scene unfold before her. An officer placed her in the back of a patrol car. One of the officers tried to talk to her, but the words sounded like whispers.

She could see the flashing lights. She had also stopped crying, but she could only sit as if frozen in place. "What have I done?" she repeated over and over.

She mustered the energy to ask the officer, "What's going to happen to him? Is my husband going to be okay? Please tell me he will be fine!" The officer offered no words in consolation. He only patted the distraught woman's back. "We can't say for sure, Ma'am."

Hilda felt her heart beating so fast that it was knocking the air out of her lungs. She couldn't breathe, and everything around her became fuzzy and blurry. Her head throbbed, and she took deep breaths to pull herself together. But the world was swimming in circles around her.

Before she knew it, she surrendered herself to the darkness and fainted.

Chapter 7
Aftermath

Adal was only five years old, and she was fatherless. She looked around at all the gloomy faces, trying to understand what was going on. She saw men dressed in suits and women in pretty black dresses. She had no way to comprehend what death meant. It broke Eva's heart to see Adal looking so confused.

"Where's daddy?" she cried. Eva held her tightly in her arms and rocked her. Adal watched her mother stare at the coffin. She was standing close to the edge of a freshly dug grave. Hilda just stood there with pale, cracked lips and bloodshot eyes. It scared Adal to see her mother look so numb.

Hilda refused to acknowledge a world in which her husband didn't exist. The person who loved her the most, her Sam, was gone. When he left, he had taken more than anyone could ever imagine. He had taken Hilda's will to live. She woke up to an empty bed. The utter loneliness would make her toss and turn.

She felt like she was the one who should have died. The guilt of her behavior was more than overwhelming. It was absolutely suffocating. There was no way that she could take any of it back. For now, Hilda was not ready to accept anything going on around her. Even the funeral felt like an elaborate lie.

"This isn't real," her mind kept telling her over and over again. It seemed like she was stuck in a nightmare. She was waiting for someone to wake her up, so she could return to her real life.

Adal's eyes that were usually so bright had been dulled by confusion. She was too young to know what was going on, but like most children, she was able to read the moods of those around her. They were all so upset. Adal could feel herself getting sadder with each passing second.

"Auntie Eva," Adal tugged Eva's hand. Eva looked down at her with tears in her eyes. "What is it?" Eva asked her kindly.

Adal pointed toward the coffin, "Why is daddy really in there?"

She asked in her small voice. Eva had told Adal that Sam was in the coffin before the funeral took place. In her immature mind, Adal thought her father was only sleeping in there.

***

It took a while for Hilda to come to her senses. Eva and the house staff took turns taking care of Adal. They didn't mind it. All of them loved her. They had mixed emotions about Hilda. Somehow, after all she had done, they still had some sympathy for her.

Hilda locked herself in her room. She went weeks, sometimes even months, without proper food. Eva was beginning to worry about her a lot. There were times when Hilda couldn't help but storm out of her room to calm her grumbling stomach. She did so one day, not knowing it was the day she would finally decide to face all that happened.

Hilda got up from her bed, put on her robe, and walked downstairs. Eva was drinking coffee and speaking to Mrs. Brizzie while Adal ate her breakfast. "Good morning, Mrs. Granger, would you like coffee and a bite of breakfast?" Mrs. Brizzie asked.

"Yes, please, whatever is leftover is fine," Hilda said and sat next to Adal.

"What are you eating?" she asked her.

"I'm having pancakes," Adal replied. "Mommy, do you like pancakes?"

"Well, I'm not sure. Can I take a bite from yours?"

Adal took a piece and poked it with her fork, and fed it to Hilda. Eva and Mrs. Brizzie just watched. Mrs. Brizzie had been pouring coffee into the cup, and it overflowed into the saucer. Hilda was aware of the eyes planted on her. She took a sip of her coffee and ate a pancake that Mrs. Brizzie put on a plate. Eva asked her how she was.

Hilda couldn't afford to hide away anymore. She wanted to pour out all the pain and hurt she felt inside. Before she could fully realize it, she was already speaking her mind, "I've made terrible mistakes in my life. I can't stop this pain from all the bad that I have I done."

Eva started to interject, "Hear me out-"

Hilda cut her off, "I'm sorry that I can't fix the past, but I can improve the future. I have a daughter that Sam loved with all his heart. I need to give him some honor, and I know I can do that by taking good care of our daughter. That would surely please him."

She was shaking a bit, and tears welled up in her eyes. She continued, "I know I have wronged him and all of you, too. I have been selfish and foolish. I was just so absorbed in my own little world that I didn't see everyone else who surrounded me. I can't get past this guilt. I did and still do love him so much."

Mrs. Brizzie could tell that the atmosphere was turning grim, so it was better to scoot Adal to her room. It was time for her to get ready for school anyway. Before Adal left the room, she ran back and gave Hilda a huge hug.

"I love you, mommy. Daddy was right."

Hilda wiped a lone tear from her eye and asked with curiosity, "Right about what?"

"He told me a long time ago to pray every night because you were sick and that you'd be better soon. You never sit at the table and talk. I'm glad that you seem better now," she smiled. The little girl kissed her mother and skipped to her room.

Hilda burst into tears. She had never cried like this before. She could hardly catch her breath and became a hiccupping mess. "Oh, Sam, what have I done? I need you. I love you," she bawled.

Eva took her in her arms, and they both cried. Mrs. Brizzie got Adal dressed for school. When they walked downstairs, Hilda went toward Adal and hunched down to her level. She said, "Mommy is very sad today, but tomorrow, Mommy would like to take you to school. Would you like that?"

Adal gave her a big hug.

After Adal left for school, the rest of the house staff continued with their chores. Eva took Hilda's hand, and they walked to the enclosed porch. The potbelly stove was cranking out the heat. They sat at the table and started to talk about how to take things from now on.

"I have the house and the college expenses ready for Adal. I don't have money for the staff, but they live here, so I will have to see if they want to stay. I have some money to live on, but until I can liquidate some of Sam's holdings, I need to be careful. He left the business to Zeke, but he's been missing in action before Adal was born," she sighed out loud.

She fiddled with the blanket on her lap, "I don't want to do anything until we know what happened to him. I know Sam would want me to continue the charity work he used to do,"

Suddenly, she closed her eyes and ran anxious glances around the room. "Oh, Eva, I can't do this! I'm so sorry! I killed him! I wanted him dead, didn't I? I don't know anymore. I just wish that it was me who died instead."

Eva just listened to Hilda cry and talk. It appeared that Hilda was finally getting to the stage of accepting Sam's death, but she was still claiming it to be her fault.

"I'm here to do whatever you need," Eva said.

"I need to work if only to occupy my mind," Hilda mentioned. "I will get a job. But first, I need to learn who my daughter is. I'm going to make Sam proud of me. It's the least I can do."

Eva nodded at her niece's heartbroken words.

Hilda took her words seriously. She was determined to bring a change in her life. She didn't want Sam's death to be in vain. He was a loving parent, and she longed to be the same. She put in the effort to become a special figure in Adal's life. It was hard at first as she would spiral around in her guilt at times, but she was doing much better.

As a year passed, she was no longer the same Hilda. Gone were the days when she pushed Adal onto the staff. She took full responsibility for her daughter.

She made her breakfast, took her to school, helped her with homework, baked her cookies, read her stories, and went to the park and zoo with her. She cuddled and listened to music with Adal before going to sleep. They bonded quickly. Hilda fell in love with that little girl, just as Sam had said she would.

She only regretted that she didn't do it while Sam was alive. Things could have been so different.

Chapter 8
Picking up The Pieces

Colleen walked outside the diner through the backdoor to get some fresh air. She paused when she saw Hilda sobbing while sitting on the steps. Her hands were drawn up to her face. Colleen hesitated momentarily but still asked, "You, alright?"

Hilda shook her head, "Yes," she replied. Colleen sat beside Hilda, removed the handkerchief from her pocket, and handed it to her. Hilda looked up at Colleen with a fake smile. She took the handkerchief, blew her nose, and wiped her face on it.

"Want this back?" She chuckled to Colleen. "Nope, all yours," Colleen shrugged. Hilda lowered her head and blew her nose in it again. "I'm sorry, I'm all good for a while, and then I don't know what comes over me. Little things just…"

"Well, it's painful to lose a husband, and it takes time," Colleen stated. Her words sounded almost monotonous. Hilda knew that Colleen was one of the few people who could relate to her.

"I know it's incredibly hard to deal with the first year of firsts. I call these the first Christmas, first birthday, first Valentine's, and all that. I remember how tough it was for me, too," she exhaled.

"Lily was not even a year old when I lost John. I recall the pain in knowing that Lily would never know or experience her father's love," Colleen opened up. She turned her head to look at Hilda. There was pain embedded in her eyes.

"I know what it feels like to lose a husband, but I also know that grief doesn't work in the same manner for everyone. I recovered because I had Lily on my mind constantly. I know that you think about your daughter, as well. You will bounce back in time."

Hilda sighed, "I try not to think about everything that happened before Sam died. I'm responsible for his death. It was my fault that he died. Sam loved me so much, but I had been blinded by everything. I just couldn't see it."

She admitted shamefully as she wiped her eyes again with her hands, "If I had known that I would lose him so early, I would have done things differently. I wish he could just come back and wake me from this nightmare."

"I know," Colleen said simply. "You know that this is the current moment. One day, you will forgive yourself. You will be okay."

Colleen stood up and extended her hand to Hilda. "Would you rather have your daughter see you crying like this? Or, would you show her that you're stronger than all of this for her sake?" she asked.

That question was more than enough to convince Hilda that Colleen was right. Hilda grabbed Colleen's hand gently and engulfed her in a tight hug as soon as she got back on her feet.

"I'm really glad that I have you, Colleen," Hilda whispered. "So am I! We're best friends, remember?" Colleen chuckled. Hilda wiped her nose clean in the handkerchief once again. After that heart to heart, she felt much better and went back to work.

The terrible guilt and shame came in waves. There were also days when she was content and relaxed and ready to move on.

As the days turned to months, Hilda felt down at times, but with each passing day, she got better. It took quite a while, but all her tears dried up.

Summer arrived. Adal spent the entire day with her mom at the diner. Lily was on summer break, so the girls would spend the whole day playing together. Adal and Lily became good friends.

On some occasions, Colleen took Adal to the farm with her. That way, Lily had a playmate for the weekend. Hilda thought it was adorable how Lily had such a protective instinct about Adal. The two children were joined at the hip. Hilda barely worried when the two of them were together.

When Hilda had to work, Adal would play with Lily all day at the diner. Aunt Eva would pick her up before it got too late. She would take her home and spent some time with her. She would ready Adal for bed, read her books, and just chat and laugh with her. Adal wished she could spend more time with Lily, but she loved "Aunt Eva nights," as she called them. Hilda was a loving and caring mother now. She worried about Adal staying up too late. She didn't want to rely on anyone to take care of Adal, and she knew that being at the diner all day wasn't good either.

The life of a single mother was hectic and busy. She tried her best to ensure she could reserve enough time for her daughter.

Hilda had her regulars at the diner. Tim Kelly was one of them. At first, she was intimidated by his tall stature, red hair, and blue eyes. He was well over six feet tall and looked as if he could lift cars all by himself. She actually blushed the first time he came in, not even wanting to take his order. She requested Colleen to do her job. However, Colleen was too busy at the counter. She insisted that Hilda take his order.

She had no idea that Tim was actually Colleen's brother. Colleen had never introduced him to her. And all the years, Colleen and Hilda were friends; Hilda never saw the farm, nor did Colleen talk much about her brothers. It was mainly because Colleen kept her private life to herself.

Hilda gathered her wits before approaching his table. She greeted him. "What can I get for you, sir?" she asked politely. She nearly had a heart attack when his light blue eyes met hers.

"I'll have the regular," he replied with a sweet smile. Hilda was giddy to hear his deep voice. It matched well with his manly figure.

"Uhm, and what would that be?" she asked him with hesitation. She was still new and had never served him before. The man seemed stunned before nodding,

"Right, I usually come in much earlier when the sun isn't even up. Sheryl is the only waitress at that time..." He stammered once he lifted his head and saw Hilda's face. A tint of red spread on his cheeks when he saw her beauty.

He handed the menu back to her. Hilda noticed his attire, "Oh, you work on a farm?" Hilda stuttered to him, hoping not to sound dumb. She found him intimidating for some reason. She wondered what had gotten into her.

"Yes, it's a few miles from here," he said. "I'm Timothy Kelly or Tim for short," he introduced himself with a faint smile.

"Oh," Hilda replied. He waited for her to tell him her name, but she just stood there. Timothy was a bit oblivious.

"I'm Hilda," she said before clearing her throat and holding the pad up to take his order. "What will you have?" she asked. Tim told her his order, not bothering to glance at the menu.

"He's a regular," Hilda thought to herself but then wondered why she had never seen him before. She figured perhaps she didn't notice him because Colleen handled most of the table customers while she worked at the counter. Now that Hilda had worked here for a few months, the owner had deemed her capable enough to work as a waitress.

Hilda approached Colleen after she took his order. She asked, "Who's that guy?"

She wanted to make a gesture toward Timothy, but she knew it would be too obvious with the way he was staring at her. "Who?" Colleen asked Hilda.

"Do you know that tall red-headed man that just came in and sat at the end of the diner?" She asked again but in a hushed voice. Colleen noticed who Hilda was referring to before giving her a wicked smile.

"Isn't he handsome?" She blurted to Hilda.

"Well, yes, he is," Hilda replied. She was not as blind as to not notice that he was indeed attractive. He seemed like a manly farmer with thickly muscled arms. He was wearing a pair of dirty overalls that reflected his profession and also donned a red and black hunting cap. Overall, he was able to capture Hilda's eye. Her heart pounded fast each time she looked at him.

She was about to ask Colleen if he was a regular before she noticed Lily walk toward the tall man's seat. "Uncle Tim," she shouted.

Hilda's eyes widened before looking back at Colleen.

"Wait, you are related to him?" She questioned, looking like a deer caught in the headlights. Colleen burst into laughter, "Yeah, that's my brother, Tim."

She laughed at Hilda, who had jerked her head back at Colleen with a flabbergasted look on her face. Hilda seemed speechless when she realized she had been tricked by her friend. They both started to chuckle. Hilda could see that Tim loved children. Adal and Lily were quite playful around him. The room was full of laughter. It was a sound that she needed to hear.

As the months passed by, Hilda always looked forward to Tim visiting the diner and ordering his usual breakfast meal. He was kindhearted and nice to Adal. He took good care of her little girl. Hilda also often talked with him whenever she could. They both hit it off and became good friends.

She had taken a liking to him, but she still carried a lot of guilt. She wanted more from this relationship, but her past was too heavy of a burden to carry. It was Eva who sensed that there was more to Hilda and Tim's friendship. She asked Hilda once who 'Uncle Tim' was as Adal had told her.

Hilda made light of it, explaining that he was a regular customer who had taken a liking to Adal. But Eva had squinted her eyes at her, feeling she was missing the big picture. Eva was right with her suspicion.

Even though Hilda never tried to admit it, it was evident with the way she smiled and gazed at Tim with stars in her eyes. They always found time for small talk while sipping coffee when Hilda was on a break, and sometimes, even when she wasn't.

She felt good around Tim. It made her happy, hearing him crack jokes and have fun with Adal and Lily. She was also impressed by how natural he was with them. He treated both his niece and Adal with equal care.

The girls looked for Tim whenever they were at the diner. Hilda was overjoyed, knowing that Adal felt as if he were her own uncle. The respect that she had for Tim kept growing. Before she knew it, she had fallen for him.

Hilda had to hold herself back. She fought the feeling. She wasn't sure whether or not Tim liked her in the same sense. Plus, Hilda didn't feel worthy of another man's love at the moment. She was afraid that she would hurt him, just like she did, Sam.

***

Tim was getting emotionally attached to Hilda. He also had some heavy thoughts. He liked his life as a single man. It didn't help that Colleen was encouraging him to pursue Hilda. Hilda had been on his mind from the first time they met at the diner. He didn't need a push. He found himself quite fond of Adal, too. He felt terrible after he heard that she had lost her father at such a young age.

Colleen was all too happy to see how interested her brother was in Hilda. She seized every opportunity she could to get this romance moving. She needed Hilda to get closer to her brother. It was all part of the big plan she had in mind.

While Adal discussed Uncle Tim with Eva, Tim discussed Hilda with Colleen. He realized it was time he became honest about his feelings and confessed to his sister that he was interested in Hilda.

"What do you like about her best?" she eagerly asked Tim. Her eyes were sparkling with excitement.

"I just have my reasons," Tim replied. "I like her, and that's all that matters. Do I really need reasons to like her?"

Colleen was pushy, and Tim didn't want to encourage her to control more of his relationship with Hilda. Yet, at the same time, he liked pushing her buttons, so he couldn't help but share this secret with her.

She rolled her eyes and said, "Okay, how about you do this? Bring Hilda and her daughter here. Show them around the farm. I'll look after the children so that you and she can have some time together. Take her out for a ride on the horses and get to know her. I know she will love the farm because she grew up in one in Germany. She told me many times that she missed it."

"I don't know... I suppose she sees me only as a friend. I don't know if she's ready for anything more. It's only been a little over a year when she lost her husband. You shouldn't push for this," he expressed his worries, but Colleen was confident that Hilda was perfect for Tim. She wanted Tim to get a life outside this farm.

"Just talk to her, Timmy," she urged him on. Tim just nodded and went off to bed. She knew that it was no use pushing her brother. She needed to give him time to let it all sink in. She knew it would. Colleen saw the way Hilda laughed with him. Her gestures and body language when she talked to him were more than enough to tell that she was in love. However, Colleen needed a plan.

She concluded that instead of driving Hilda and Adal home as she did sometimes. She could make an excuse to stop at the farm. She didn't think either Hilda or Tim would mind. Colleen paced around the room in excitement. She couldn't wait for what the future had in store. Every day, she stood smiling at Hilda, who laughed at yet another one of Tim's corny jokes. They hit it off so well. Anyone could see that spark between them.

They talked and talked at coffee breaks. Though they didn't have formal dates, the diner did the trick. They even had long telephone conversations for hours. Colleen whistled out loud, content with the way things were going. Hilda, who could appreciate the love in her life, and Tim, who was stuck on this farm for hours – Colleen was certain

they needed to be together. She was ready to do all she could
to let their love lives blossom.

Chapter 9
Simple Life

Timothy was a simple man. He had never thought much about dating because he had his church and family. The love that he had for God and his family had always been enough for him. Tim believed that he could never love anyone more than he loved his sister and niece.

However, everything changed when Hilda walked into his life. Tim felt overly self-conscious when he first met her. He was a farmer who worked day and night in the dirty fields while she was a beautiful woman. Hilda seemed to be on his mind all the time.

He thought that his family was complete because he had Colleen and Lily. But now, he was starting to grow very fond of Hilda and her child. His feelings for Hilda were different, though. His heart raced, and his palms would turn sweaty whenever he thought of her. He found himself smiling a lot more these days. He daydreamed about her beauty. Her brownish red curls, heart-shaped face, and soft brown eyes took his breath away every time.

"I hope I don't smell like the barn…Well, thank God, I at least got a haircut. Oh no, is she looking my way?" These were the thoughts that went through his mind the very first time he met Hilda. He first took a glimpse at the beautiful girl over the top of his menu as his sister talked with her at the diner. He tried to act discretely that day, not too sure whether he had succeeded.

It was hard for Tim not to be hopeful each time Hilda's cheeks blushed bright pink when they saw each other. His heart would literally skip a beat whenever Hilda gave him the slightest encouragement.

Tim liked everything about Hilda, especially how she expressed her love for Adal. He remembered the advice his brother Jason had given him, "Smile. Make them laugh and be polite," he had said. They often talked about dating when Jason was home.

How he wished that his brother was here now! Jason was the good looking one who was never without a girl. Tim, on the other hand, was not confident like him. Tim had been told he was handsome, but he never really gave it much thought.

He was not insecure, but looks weren't that important to him. He liked down to earth people like those in church. He liked having deep talks with someone and knowing their personality instead of gawking over their physical beauty. He found most women to be shallow, not that he believed all of them to be. The ones he met were just not for him. Tim had never even approached a girl. It was quite the other way around.

The girls at school would approach him and ask him out on a date. He would always turn them down. He suspected that they were only trying to get close to Jason. All the girls wanted to date Jason, who was charming and attractive.

Though he was intrigued by Hilda's beauty, he also found her to be a real and honest person. She was down to earth, and it gave him goosebumps. He knew there was more to her than met the eye. She had a big heart and a broken soul. He could tell that she was struggling with some hardships in her life. And one day, he decided to ask Colleen about it.

"Hilda has been your friend for a long time. Tell me about her?" Tim asked Colleen while having lunch at the diner. But Colleen only shook her head, "It's not my place to tell. I think that it's better if you ask her yourself."

She was hoping Tim could have an emotional conversation with Hilda that would drive them into each other's arms.

"Come on, sis, tell me something!" He pleaded. Colleen was enjoying this. She taunted him, "You like her, don't cha?" Tim paused. He averted his gaze as if he were considering the possibility.

"She's married, isn't she!?" Tim worried out loud, surprised to hear himself sound so jealous. He had never felt like that before.

"No, stupid," Colleen retorted as she sat opposite to him. "Hilda is not married."

"What do you mean by that?" Tim asked her.

Colleen just rolled her eyes at his oblivious personality. She explained, "Hilda is a widow. We have been friends since high school."

She proceeded to tell him about Hilda's life. It was upsetting for him to know that Hilda had once suffered so much pain. But he was surprised at just how relieved he felt, knowing that she was widowed. "If you were friends since high school, how come you never brought her around?" He asked her.

"Are you kidding, little brother? With grandpa and you always preaching Jesus, and this dirty old place..." she sighed but immediately wished that she hadn't worded it so badly.

Tim didn't respond. He knew that Hilda was happy when she saw him interact with the kids. What he didn't know was how giddy she was to see how fond he was of her. He had unveiled a part of her life and felt guilty for doing that behind her back. He wished that there was a different way to get even closer to her. He wanted more than just deep conversations with Hilda.

Tim was pleased when Colleen would bring both Hilda and Adal to the farm on the way home, even if it were for a brief moment. He was ready to take the next step. Tim planned a picnic with Hilda, Adal, Colleen, and Lily. He knew that Colleen would give him some space, and Lily would keep Adal busy. It was the perfect way for him to talk to Hilda alone. Still, he felt so nervous.

He walked into the diner after mustering up his courage. The bell on the door jingled when he entered. Hilda looked up at the entrance as if she had anticipated his arrival. Tim grinned at her, but before he could take a step toward her, he looked down to see Adal and Lily wrapping their arms on his legs.

"Uncle Tim! Uncle Tim!" They crowded around him as if he were a celebrity.

"Oh, hey, kiddos!" Tim greeted them as he scooped both Lily and Adal up in his arms with ease.

Hilda laughed as Adal exclaimed happily, "Woah! Uncle Tim is so strong!"

Lily wrapped her arms around Tim's neck, "See, I told you my uncle Tim is strong. He can also pick up Shadow with me in his arms."

"Who's Shadow?" Adal asked innocently as Hilda escorted them to a table.

"My dog," Lily informed Adal with pride.

Adal's eyes widened. She said excitedly, "The black one?"

Tim sat down with both the children in his lap. "Uh-huh," said Lily.

"Really, I can show you the new puppies if your mom wants to come to a picnic on Saturday," Tim told them as he looked up at Hilda.

Adal pleaded, "Mom, can we please visit the puppies at Uncle Tim's farm?"

Tim's heart thumped fast in his chest as he waited for Hilda's answer.

"I...I don't think that is appropriate," Hilda replied in a stutter before she took out her writing pad and pen. All of a sudden, she seemed really overwhelmed.

"Why not?" Tim spoke up. "We talked about it the other night on the telephone. You sounded like you really wanted to have the grand tour."

"I don't want to burden you, Tim," she said. She changed the subject quickly, "Uhm, may I know what you would like to order today?"

"Mom, please!" Adal requested again with a pouty face. Hilda didn't want to deny Adal's request every time she asked for something. She really wanted to go herself, too.

She was in a quandary. Was this going to lead her heart down a path that she didn't want to go? Many thoughts were racing in her head at once. Hilda was suddenly reminded of Sam, and it pained her. She felt as if she had been kicked in the stomach.

"No, we can't go," she firmly said. The words were hurtful to say out loud. She turned away, unable to withstand her aching stomach. Colleen watched as Hilda rushed past the counter. Her brother looked puzzled.

Colleen approached the table. She was glad that the diner was nearly empty tonight. "I don't know what happened," Tim expressed his concern as soon as his sister sat next to him. Colleen looked at Adal and could see that the child was just as heartbroken as Tim.

"I think that it's better for you kids to go play for a while," Colleen suggested. Lily pouted, but she dragged Adal with her off to another part of the diner.

"Can you please check on her?" Tim requested. Colleen just shook her head. "First, I need you to tell me what just happened here." She crossed her arms.

Tim tried to explain everything before asking his sister what he had done wrong. Colleen smacked her forehead as she grabbed her brother by the shoulders.

"You can't do that, Tim. What were you thinking?" Colleen stated firmly. "You can't use the child to manipulate Hilda into accepting your invitation. You're not talking to one of your dumb animals. You should have asked her when she was alone. Can't you see that she can never say 'no' to Adal? Hilda doesn't want to hurt her child's feelings. You must go out there and explain to her that you wanted to invite her to visit the farm for a long time now. Go tell her!" Colleen advised and patted him on the shoulder.

He took a deep breath as he rose from the table. "You are not going to mess this up for me," Colleen mumbled to herself. She told Tim where to find Hilda. He headed toward the backside of the diner but hesitated when he saw Hilda leaning against the far wall with her head bowed. She looked up at him as the door creaked shut behind him. Tim felt his heart twinge in pain when he noticed the tears in her eyes.

Her face was red from crying, and she looked away. "I look pathetic. Don't I?" She sniffled as she took a deep breath while staring up at the sky.

"No, you don't," Tim bit his lip in worry. Hilda shook her head. "Yes, I do. I am pathetic, Tim. I am," Hilda cut herself off before she locked her swollen eyes with him. "I ran away from Adal because she's been through so much that I hate to refuse her..." she said in a whisper and wiped the tears off her face with both hands. "I'm sorry for what I did," Tim apologized sincerely.

Hilda shook her head at him. "Why? You don't need to," she wept. Tim understood what Colleen had been talking about. Tim could see both the sweetness and sadness in Hilda, and it only made him feel more protective of her than ever.

"It was wrong of me to ask you that in front of the children. I didn't mean to put you in that position, Hilda. I should have asked you when we were alone. I've been planning on asking you to go out with me for a while now," Tim explained himself.

He gulped before saying, "Not just the farm, but ...you know, a date. Like a regular date with you as my girlfriend." Tim admitted to his feelings with a defeated look, thinking that she wouldn't take his offer. Not after what had happened! He was devastated for ruining his chance.

"You were planning on asking me out as a girlfriend....?" She questioned. She was focused on him, waiting for a reply.

"Yes, I have been planning on it for a while now. Is that bad?" Tim stared at the ground, immediately regretting how he sounded. His palms were sweaty, and he could hear his heart beating loudly. He was sure she could hear it, too. He had wanted to tell Hilda how he felt for so long. He wanted to be a little romantic, give her flowers when he asked her, but things turned out differently.

"Oh. It's…I mean…" Hilda was trying to find the right words to explain herself to him.

Tim made up his mind to just spit it out and ask her, "Would you like to come out to the farm, see the puppies, and go on a picnic with us all?"

He added, "I can show you and Adal the new litter. Colleen will be there, too. We can have a little picnic near the lake. There are so many beautiful places up there, as well. It will be like a day trip." Tim spoke quickly to cover up the fact that he was asking her out in an alleyway. Hilda seemed relieved, but she was still hesitating a little. "I don't know if it's alright. You're a great friend, Tim, and I don't want to trouble you," she frowned.

He comforted her, "No, it won't be troubling me at all! I'm a patient man, Hilda, take all the time you need. Just don't tell Colleen that I said that. She wants us married by tomorrow and living in the city."

They both started laughed. "We can delay the marriage to the following week." Tim joked. Hilda blushed as she thought about it for a moment. Tim leaned his head down a little to stare into her gorgeous eyes. Hilda felt as if her breath was stuck somewhere in her throat. She gazed directly into his clear blue eyes.

"I really want to show you and Adal around the farm. I would enjoy that. The farm is a part of my life, and I would like to share it with you," he moved his hand up to stroke her hair but stopped. "Plus, you'll get to have a break yourself. You won't have to do anything except enjoy the picnic."

Hilda nodded, and Tim cheered, almost hugging Hilda. "That's great!" He beamed as he thought about proposing to Hilda in the meadow. "Slow down now," he whispered to himself. He knew Hilda was the only woman for him.

"You're sure that it will be fine?" She asked once more.

"Of course!" Tim joyfully responded. He gave her a hug this time and a small kiss on the forehead. He noticed her heart beating fast. They continued to talk for a few more minutes outside. Tim offered to pick Hilda and Adal up at the diner on Saturday since Hilda got off early that day. She suggested something else, "Nien, come to my house. I'm taking a day off, so come early."

Tim was beyond happy. He told her a bit about his life on the farm since Hilda had never really seen it. She found her anxious heart easing bit by bit. Suddenly, she found herself laughing out loud, all within the span of a few minutes. It was as if a wave of cool water had washed over her and took all her stress away.

Hilda went back inside the diner, only after Colleen peeked out the door to check on them. Tim followed after a few minutes with a wide grin on his face. He was delighted knowing Hilda had agreed to visit the farm. He quickly reflected on the entire conversation he and Hilda had just had. He valued her openness and honesty. He knew that she was struggling with guilt and agonized about her late husband. He might not know everything about her past, but truly, he didn't care.

This was here and now. All he cared about was who Hilda really was now. It didn't matter what she did in the past. "Do not call to mind the former things, or ponder things of the past," he repeated the scripture in his head.

Lily and Adal crowded around Tim again after they spotted him emerging from the back of the diner. He picked Adal up in his arms and grinned at her. "Why the long face, sweetheart?" He asked her.

"I want to see the puppies," Adal mumbled as she peeked at her mom, who was busy making plans with Colleen.

"Did you talk to my mom?" She whispered to him while cupping her hands over Tim's ear. "Yes, I did," he whispered back, even though no one was there to hear it anyways. It was just too cute not to. "What did she say?" She whispered again.

"She said that you guys are going to visit our farm this weekend."

Adal screeched happily, wiggling out of his arms. She ran and hugged her mother tightly. "Oh, thank you, mommy!" Adal cried out to her. "Can I play with the puppies?"

Hilda nodded as she patted her little girl's head, "Yes, yes, you may."

"Yay! I'm going to play at your farm, Lily!" Adal smiled and jumped around happily. The two girls hugged and danced in circles. Colleen scolded the children and asked them to keep it down while they were in the diner. Hilda mouthed the words, "Thank you," to Tim. He wondered what she was thanking him for; then, it hit him.

Hilda was thanking him for making Adal happy. Tim gave her a firm nod and ruffled his hair with a wide smile before Hilda got back to work. He went back to his seat and sighed in relief.

Colleen passed Tim a small smile and held a thumb up before she headed back to work, as well. Tim chuckled at her and watched Hilda filling the saltshakers over at the counter. The diner was nearly empty. Tim ate his dinner slowly, so he could be around Hilda and the kids.

It had gotten late, and he left for home, all satisfied and joyous. Tim had so much work to do, yet he wasn't letting that put him in a bad mood. He was thankful that he had hired help at the farm. Right now, nothing bothered him. A lot of happy and gleeful thoughts came to him. But the one thing he pondered over the most was confessing his love to Hilda.

He wanted to tell Hilda that he was madly in love with her. She needed to hear it clearly from him. He drove back home with his head in the clouds and his heart dancing to a joyful beat.

Chapter 10
Farm Day

Hilda could tell how excited Adal was to visit the farm and see the puppies. She watched Adal run through the house, telling everyone about the picnic.

The pure excitement was music to Hilda's ears. Her thoughts drifted back to Sam. Though the guilt was still there about how she had treated him, she was at peace as they had cleared their misunderstanding. She knew that Sam would be so pleased to see the progress that she had made in her relationship with Adal.

She still mourned about what could have been if she were a better wife and mother. She tempered those regrets with the respect that she had for Sam's integrity. He was truly a great man.

Through Tim and his faith, Hilda was beginning to understand that she could forgive herself. She knew she could only honor Sam by loving Adal and that she did. Adal was a true blessing to Hilda and a source of great healing. Hilda was also thankful for the two ladies in their house who cared for Adal. Those women had no place to go, and they truly loved Adal. They had both decided to continue working as housemaids in exchange for a room. It was working out quite well. The house itself was debt-free; Sam had seen to that. The money he had left for the house's expenses had proved sufficient for making ends meet. However, Mrs. Wheeler wasn't with them anymore.

She had left to care for another family. She was discontent living with Hilda. She just couldn't seem to find any grace in her heart for Hilda. It was, as they say, for the best. Hilda made sure to give her a reference because she cared for Mrs. Wheeler, despite their bitter relationship.

Finally, it was a Saturday, the day of the picnic. Hilda was folding the clothes Adal left on the bed. Adal was picking out an outfit for the much anticipated day. "Mommy, what do you think of these?" Adal asked, pointing to her blue jeans and sneakers.

Hilda swallowed hard. Guilt welled up inside her, but she managed a smile for her daughter. Sam had bought that outfit for her just over a year ago. The shoes were too big then, but they fitted her perfectly now. Mrs. Brizzie put her hair in pigtails and added a red ribbon that matched her red and white checked shirt.

"You look adorable!" Hilda patted her head. She meant it. Adal looked like a walking doll with her gorgeous curly hair tied and pink, puffy cheeks.

"What about Mommy? Does she look nice, too?" Hilda asked her daughter as she checked out her deep green shirt and blue jeans that she had just purchased at Delson's Dept. Store yesterday. Hilda had to admit that she felt good wearing them.

Adal just hugged her mother around her waist and smiled. "You look pretty, Mom," Adal praised with a huge smile across her face. It had been a while since Hilda picked out her best clothes and got dressed. She felt more like herself. She didn't have to pretend to be anyone else anymore this time. Sam used to constantly reassure her that he didn't marry her to conform to societal norms. Still, she never felt quite comfortable.

He always said that it was her natural beauty that made him fall in love with her. She, however, never quite saw it that way. The crowd that they associated with never seemed to acknowledge her. Now thinking back on it, she remembered a flannel shirt Sam loved wearing at home. She smiled to herself as she reminisced fondly about Sam. She lightly slapped her cheeks and stared at herself in the mirror.

"I can do this. It'll be fine. I'm okay. Colleen is going to be there, too. It's going to be okay," she repeated to calm herself.

Tim picked up Hilda and Adal from the house early in the morning, as promised. "You look great," Tim said, eyeing Hilda's outfit. She showed a shy smile, which meant she enjoyed the compliment. The awkward silence that followed was broken when Adal jumped into Tim's arms. "Good morning, little one. You look gorgeous as always, sweetheart." Tim pulled out his fake southern accent that always made Adal laugh out loud. Hilda joined in the laughter. Thankfully, the tension was broken.

They hopped into Tim's old truck that he loved so much. Adal sat between Tim and Hilda with a picnic basket on her lap. Hilda had taken the liberty of preparing snacks for the picnic, even though Colleen had told her not to. It was the least that Hilda could do. She had prepared some egg sandwiches and peanut butter and jelly sandwiches for the girls. Tim and Hilda used the time together to talk to each other casually. Adal interrupted at regular intervals, but everyone was having a great time.

"Mommy, look at the horse over there...look at that silly..." Adal kept pointing at the animals they passed by. She exclaimed upon seeing every new animal. Tim's heart was full. He told Adal some fun facts about the different animals and joked along the way. Adal felt special, sitting between her mother and her favorite uncle.

She couldn't wait to see Lily again. But leaving everything aside, she wanted to play with those puppies. Adal got more excited as they drove down the dusty dirt roads that lead to the farm. She could see many green fields, flowers, and open skies. Even Hilda was struck by the view that greeted them. Hilda allowed her long hair to flow with the wind as she stuck her head out of the window. The cool breeze met her face. The skies were blue and beautiful. For the first time in a long while, Hilda felt free.

She allowed her eyes to close and feel the breeze against her face. The sunlight was seeping down into her skin. Adal climbed in her lap. Hilda carefully balanced her weight, and both looked out of the window, enjoying the beauty of the moment.

At that moment, Hilda felt liberated from the weight of all the sorrows that were holding her down. The panging grief that weighed so heavily on her chest had finally lifted. It was like redemption.

Hilda was not a widow or a grieving single mother today. No, she was Tim and Colleen's greatest friend. As they arrived at the farm, Hilda suddenly felt as if she were back home in Germany with Mama and Papa. A wholesomeness flooded over her. She felt as though after a very long time, she could breathe freely.

She listened to the sound of nature. She breathed in the smell of the farm. She loved that smell, which most found to be pungent. It reminded her of home. She closed her eyes and heard her father calling out to her. She sensed that he was at peace where he was. She felt Mama's warm cheek against her. Hilda was at peace.

Tim parked the truck near a big red clapboard house that had a front porch wrapped halfway around the entire home. Colleen had brought them by the house a few times after work, but they never got out of the car to see it up close. Colleen and Lily were already standing in the middle of the porch when Tim pulled up with Hilda and Adal.

Hilda went to greet Colleen while Adal and Lily hugged each other tightly and did their circle dance. Lily grabbed Adal's hand and led her to the barn to see the puppies. Colleen told her to play with the puppies after lunch. But they had already reached the barn when they were stampeded by little black balls of fluff.

"We can have our lunch near the lake," Tim suggested.

Colleen seemed delighted with the idea. "Oh, yes, the lake has the most wonderful view," she said and grabbed Hilda's hand. "You can take care of the kids, Tim. Hilda and I will pack lunch. Come on, Hilda."

Colleen dragged Hilda away before Tim could say anything. He watched the two ladies walk away. He shrugged and headed toward the barn.

"Alright, who's ready to play catch?" he screamed to the kids. Their laughter filled the barn. All the little puppies, six of them, crawled over both the girls, who were laughing and screaming with excitement.

"He's awfully good with kids, isn't he?" Colleen elbowed Hilda as she added her sandwiches next to the food Hilda had prepared.

"It was surprising to me at first when I saw Tim taking such good care of Lily after she was born. One would think that he would want to get married as soon as possible and have lots of children around." Colleen mentioned carefully, trying to gauge Hilda's reaction.

Collen wasn't concerned with Tim having children. She hoped to see him get married already. That comment definitely caught Hilda's attention, and she looked back at Colleen. "Is that so? Does he have anyone in mind?" She asked Colleen, a little too curiously. She knew how Collen doesn't share her private matters often, so she didn't probe further.

"Don't be silly." Colleen rolled her eyes, knowing that she was caught in her own net. "Only Timothy knows what's going on in that head of his. Here, keep this in your basket and let's go," Colleen wrapped up the conversation, hoping things didn't turn awkward, and headed out of the house and waved at the trio. "Timmy? Kids? Let's go to the lake!" She shouted at them.

Adal and Lily came running over. They were out of breath and covered in hay. Hilda laughed at their flushed cheeks before wiping the dirt from Adal's face. "Look at you. Are you having fun?" Hilda asked her. Adal nodded eagerly with excitement in her eyes.

"Good, so am I," Hilda winked at Adal. All of them walked toward the edge of the farm, following the path until they came across the lake. The water seemed to shine like crystals under the sun, and the breeze was surprisingly warm.

Colleen laid out a blanket on the ground under a nice tree near the lake. Adal and Lily sat on either side of Tim as Colleen and Hilda handed them plates and sandwiches. Adal and Lily finished quickly. They were more eager to explore.

Hilda, Colleen, and Tim were engrossed in a conversation that was interrupted by the kids. Lily wrapped her arms around her Uncle Tim's neck from behind. "Let's go and show Adal around, Uncle Tim! We can even have a pony ride," Lily exclaimed.

Colleen knew that Tim wanted to be alone with Hilda for a while, so she decided to show the girls around herself. "Come on, girls, come with me. You'll be fine here, right, Hilda?" she looked back at Hilda. Hilda nodded, "Of course," Adal came over and kissed Hilda's cheek before she went over to Colleen.

"Do you really have a pony, Lily?" Adal asked as they walked away from the lake. Hilda and Tim glanced at each other for a moment before Hilda turned her head to stare at the lake. "This place is so beautiful," she whispered with a small smile.

Tim looked at her face. The sun glowed off her cheeks, and the more he stared, the more he realized that she was indeed breathtaking. "I agree," Tim replied.

Hilda turned toward Tim, "My father owned a farm as well, and I spent my childhood playing around in the mud."

He was surprised to hear that, "I thought you were from the city." Colleen had told him she knew of the farm life, but he never believed much of what Colleen said. She was always spicing things up. Hilda shook her head, "It is complicated to explain, but my father owned farmland back in Germany. We prospered for a while until he was betrayed by one of the landlords to the Nazi's. They seized his farm, and we were forced to move."

She glanced at the swaying trees, "Farms in Germany were not as beautiful as the farms here, but it still reminds me of home. Truth be told, it reminds me of the place that I am trying desperately not to forget. This is where I truly came from. For the longest time, I had tried to fit in with the crowd here in America."

She didn't know why she was suddenly telling him everything, but she didn't regret it. Tim sat without saying a word, focusing entirely on her.

She went on, "People here fascinated me so much that I started hating who I really was, and where I actually came from. The war, of course, made it so much worse. I am so ashamed of what Germany did. I am angry that I lost my family. I wrote them during the war, but my letters were never returned. I hated Germany, Tim."

Tim's heart broke for Hilda. At that moment, he learned that he loved her even more. He drew close to her and looked into her eyes as if asking for permission. She nodded and tenderly grabbed his hand to pull him closer. They kissed, then pulled back immediately. Just like that, they kissed once more. "I love you, Hilda," he said softly.

Hilda felt her heart leap out of her chest. They both drowned in the beauty of the crystal water as Hilda's back was cupped into Tim's chest. His arms were folded in front of her chest. She could feel his warm breath on the back of her neck.

"I love you too, Tim," she replied.

Hearing that, he just couldn't wait anymore. "Marry me," he blurted out.

Hilda turned to face Tim. "I'm not a fancy man. I'm not a big spender. I'm a humble man of God. I love my farm, my animals, and my Savior. If you can love all that, I want you to be with me for the rest of my life. My heart can't take much more. I see you, and I don't know what happens to me. I pray for you every day. I don't care about your past because I think you are who you were meant to be now."

He caressed her hands, "I want to be Adal's father. I want to be your husband. I love you so very much."

Tim touched her face, wiping away the tears that ran down Hilda's cheeks. She stammered, "I want to say yes, Tim. I want to say yes."

He knew what she meant. He brushed off the hair strand stuck to her lipstick, "I will wait as long as I need to. There is no one else for me."

The picnic ended with these heartfelt words. Adal enjoyed the trip so much that she persuaded Hilda to go again next week. Hilda laughed and reassured they would come back soon. She was in a daze in the car on their way home. Adal slept on her mother's lap. It was a quiet ride home.

Chapter 11
Something's Wrong with Colleen

Eva stopped by Hilda's house to inform her of some great news. Hilda put on a pot of coffee, and Eva sat down at the kitchen table. Hilda pulled out some sugar cookies from the bread box and removed the wax paper. She put them on the plate. Adal came running in and grabbed one before Hilda could stop her.

"Young lady? Where are your manners? Say hello to Auntie Eva," she scolded. Adal did as her mother instructed and gave her auntie a big hug. She was covered in cookie crumbs that clung onto Eva's hair and dress after the hug, so she laughed.

Eva brushed the crumbs off and gathered them in her hands; then, she threw them away in a garbage can behind her. She sat back down. Eva cared a lot about cleaning and keeping things tidy.

Lately, she passed the time by dusting the house or sorting out her stuff. Hilda put the cookies on the table and extracted cream from the refrigerator. She was planning on preparing some sweets for her guest. Just then, Adal ran off full speed to the playroom. "Oh, she wears me out," Hilda laughed with an audible breath.

Eva agreed, "She is a little rascal."

"Honestly, I don't know what I would do without her. She's been my lifeline since Sam passed," Hilda said and poured coffee into two mugs.

"How are you doing? I haven't seen you in a bit," Eva asked.

Hilda smiled, "I'm actually doing well. I've made peace with Sam's passing, and my relationship with Adal is growing nicely. Enough about that for now. What's your big news?"

Eva wasted no time to exclaim, "Haversmith's Furniture Store hired me!" She clasped her hands together in glee, "I have full-time hours in the office, and I get a commission if I sell any furniture. You want a new sofa?"

Hilda laughed, "I inherited the house but not the wealth. It all goes to Adal when she turns eighteen. I don't deserve any of it. I kept a small amount to pay the taxes and utilities.

A cozy sofa does sound great, though."

"I'll be glad to have regular payments that can help me move out of that trailer. It served its purpose, and I'm ready to move forward," Eva heaved a sigh. It had been years living in that trailer, and she wanted a better life for herself now.

"I have an idea, Aunt Eva!" Hilda exclaimed all of a sudden. "Why don't you move in here? We have plenty of room. Doesn't that sound like a great idea? I wonder why I didn't think of it before."

Eva thought of the possibility, "What about Mrs. Brizzie and Mrs. Murphy?"

With a shrug of shoulders, Hilda replied, "What about them? They have their own rooms and live here in exchange for housekeeping and helping with Adal. They won't mind you being here. They love you. Your added income can also help us all, plus you'd have a nice place to live."

Hilda added between giggles, "You can even have a puppy...."

"Hmmm... that is actually not a bad idea," Eva considered her options. She did want a change. She had been working hard and applying for different jobs for a while now. This new job was her big break.

Mr. Haversmith's son had hired her to help with bookkeeping and working on the floor sales. Since the economy was doing so well, the sales were more than expected. She was offered a much better salary than her previous job.

The idea of owning a pet dog was intriguing to Eva. She chuckled, "A puppy! Oh, I want one. If it is a girl, I will name her Betti Boop, or if it's a male, then I'll call him Cooper after dreamy Gary Cooper. Do you know someone with puppies?"

Hilda leaned back, "I do, and I'm sure he would give you one. He's a nice person, after all. Well, let's think about it. Once you get here, you may have more room. You will also need…"

She trailed off. She couldn't seem to gather her thoughts as if a sudden memory distracted her. Hilda poured more coffee in their cups and stayed silent. "You okay?" Eva questioned.

"Oh, Eva, I'm in a quandary. I don't know what to do!

Order wohin man sich wenden kann..." Hilda switched to German whenever she was in a pinch, nervous, or overwhelmed. Both of them started to speak in half English and half German to each other before realizing it. Hilda broke the chain, "English only, or we will never have a friend here."

She worked on her accent a lot, and it showed with the way she spoke English so fluently now. Her accent would creep in sometimes, but she was determined to fix it and fit in.

Eva noticed that Hilda was clearly hiding something from her. "You know you can talk to me anytime. I may not have been such a great maternal figure for you in the past, but you helped me find myself. I want you to know that."

She folded her hands in front of her and leaned in on the table, and looked directly at Hilda. "So, what's the problem?"

Hilda felt silly. "It's nothing major..." she went on, but her voice was fading. She breathed out and blurted, "I got proposed to last week."

Eva stood up, "What?! Who? I knew something was up with you when I didn't hear from you."

"You remember Tim from the diner? You know Colleen's brother?"

"Yes!"

Hilda gulped and smiled shyly, "Well, Colleen introduced us, and we've been dating now."

She went on, "He owns Redtop Farm in Tarrytown. Adal loves it there. His dog has a lot of puppies. That was why I brought it up. Adal wants to keep them all."

She laughed a little and took a sip of the warm coffee. Eva was full of questions, "He's good to you and Adal? It is a lot to take on a woman with another man's child, you know?"

"I know, but he loves us both very much. But there is an issue,"

"What do you mean?" Eva asked.

"Sam!"

Eva shook her head back and forth as if she were puzzled. "Sam? Sam...I don't get it."

"I was so awful to Sam. How can I just replace him? It's not fair to him," Hilda choked out the words.

"How is it not fair to Sam? He's dead!" Eva responded.

"I know. That is true, but I can't make it up to him. To be happy after what I did just isn't right," Hilda began to cry.

Eva locked eyes with Hilda, "Did you even know Sam? He was the most forgiving, kind, and loving man I ever saw. I am sure you remember what he did for those families that suffered during the war. He held those employees' jobs until they got back. The man that loved you through your pregnancy and post-pregnancy trauma? He is the same Sam that loved you to the end. Sam wants what is best for Adal and you. He wouldn't want to see you so broken."

Hilda wiped her tears, "I guess you're right."

"Do you love Tim?"

"Yes," Hilda admitted. "He's a lot like Sam but in many different ways. Does that make sense?"

"Perfectly, but please remember that Sam forgave you," Eva rubbed Hilda's back to comfort her.

Hilda stared at the ground and said, "Did he? Because I killed him, didn't I?"

"Yes, he loved you. So, when can I move in?" Eva broke the tension. They both chuckled. Eva stood up and hugged Hilda tightly. "I'm sorry I wasn't a great influence on you at first, but you turned out pretty darn great."

Hilda hugged back and replied joyfully, "Let's go rob my closet for some dresses for your new job."

"I thought you'd never ask," Eva joked.

Hilda found five dresses that she had never worn. She also found shoes, purses, and even hats to match. She loved those dresses, but she no longer felt like they represented who she was. She handed it all to Eva, and after another tight hug, they said their goodbyes.

***

Colleen had assumed that Hilda had said 'yes' to Tim when he proposed. Tim was not acting any different. He was humming while he worked, laughed with Lily, and seemed to be his old self.

Lily had spent the night at Tim's because Colleen had worked the night shift. They had moved away from the farm and settled back in the city as Colleen was now financially stable enough to do so. She went to pick up Lily at Tim's after the breakfast rush. She needed to know more about what went down during that picnic. "So, Tim, what's the date?" She pried.

"For what?" he teased.

She was always nosey about her brother's matters and wanted to squeeze them out of him. Tim was okay with Hilda needing time to think about his proposal because he knew she would eventually say 'yes.'

"You and Hilda," Colleen replied.

"Oh, that," he took a sip of his coffee and put the mug down on the porch table. He picked up his bible and began to read how Jacob's love for Rachel was so grand that he worked and waited seven years for her. Colleen was getting impatient. "Did you ask her or not?" She pleaded.

"I did," he answered just to continue annoying her. "I'm reading a great love story right now. Grab a cup of coffee, and I'll read it to you," he knew, dragging this out would drive her insane.

"I don't want coffee! What is wrong with you? Can't you be nice?" Colleen said with petulance. She almost shouted, "Honestly, Tim, I'll never be able to get you off this damn farm!"

Tim's ears perked up. "What?" He mumbled. "We are not going to go through this again. I have told you before that this is my home, and when I leave, I will be in a pine box. Then I want to be buried in the ground under the big maple." He replied sternly.

"Well, what if Hilda wants to move?" she asked.

"No need to concern yourself with that. She said no."

Colleen's eyes widened, "Excuse me? NO! She said NO!"

Colleen left Lily in the barn and jumped in the car to drive away. Tim just laughed to himself. He knew it was just her regular habit of wanting to control everything. He turned to see that Lily was still there. "I think you forgot something…" his voice trailed off as he laughed out loud at his sister's clumsiness. He shook his head and went back to his bible.

***

Hilda was chopping some fruit in the kitchen to make a light snack for Adal. She was relieved after having a talk with Eva. Now, she knew her answer to Tim's proposal.

With Eva moving into the house and the other two ladies maintaining it, there would be no need to sell the house. She can keep it for Adal. Thankfully, things were turning out for the best, and she hadn't been deeply stressed and worried for a while now.

She was meeting Tim tonight and was ready to tell him her answer. While washing up the dishes, there was a knock on the front door. Hilda checked and saw Colleen outside. Once she opened the door, Colleen came barreling in. She yelled at Hilda, "What is your issue!"

Hilda was taken aback, so she said, "What in tarnation got your feathers in flight?"

"You rejected his proposal? How could you say NO? Tim needs you. Don't you understand! He needs to get off that farm and sell it," she stopped herself before she let out all the thoughts in her head.

"You'll ruin my whole plan if you don't marry him," she sighed to herself. Hilda didn't know that Colleen still hated that farm with a passion. Colleen thought the value of that land was just being wasted with the way it was right now. She wanted her share, especially after her husband's death and going through financial troubles. She felt cheated.

"I only said no because..." Colleen cut Hilda off mid-sentence. "You are selfish and awful, and you will....you know what? Never mind." Colleen turned around and left as fast as she came in.

Hilda didn't know what to think. Colleen seemed insane. She picked up the phone to call Meg, but the line was in use. Meg would know what was wrong with Colleen. Meg was much calmer and thought out things better; she was not hot-headed like Colleen. Colleen was often impulsive, and while it was fun when they were young, it was quite destructive now.

Finally, the phone was clear.

"Operator, get me riverside 5070, please."

The phone connected to Meg. Hilda's face brightened up, "Hello, Meg? Yes, it's me, Hilda. How have you been?"

Hilda sat on the bed, hoping to get a little more information about Colleen's attitude. But they started to catch up on their lives.

"That's grand! When's the wedding.....well, I'll definitely be there. Meg, honey, can we meet sometime soon? Thursday is fine. Can you come here? Great! I'll have lunch ready. See you then. Bye."

Meg told her that she was marrying her fiancé, Paul, next month, so Hilda didn't get a chance to ask her about Colleen. Hearing exciting news was always fun. Hilda ran upstairs to check up on Adal and get dressed for her date with Tim. They were going into town for a cinema date to see Key Largo with Humphrey Bogart as Tim was a huge Bogart fan.

She wanted to tell him about her decision today.

Chapter 12
Married Life

After asking Meg to visit her place and talk about Colleen, Hilda prepared a feast. They were reuniting after so many months. It would be a breath of fresh air for both.

Hilda asked about whatever was worrying Colleen, and what she heard from Meg startled her. She found out that Colleen was in a financial pinch and wanted to sell the land.

Hilda marched straight to Colleen's place the next day to clarify the misunderstanding. Once Colleen opened the door, Hilda hugged her. "I am so sorry. I knew nothing," she whispered.

Colleen was unresponsive at first, but then she hugged back. She never showed her soft side to people, but she still hugged Hilda back at the moment. She lowered her gaze, "Nah, it's me who should be sorry. I was selfish. I just......"

Colleen looked down, "I was also too pushy with you two. I thought he would sell the land if he met you. You both could move into the city, but I guess not."

Hilda rubbed her back, "Don't worry too much. You can rely on us always! I said no to him because I was unprepared. You know how Sam is still lurking in my mind. But I love Tim. I think I can't fathom letting someone else take him away from me."

She added with a broken voice, "I want to live the rest of my life with him. I have decided. I love him so very much, Colleen. I don't think you understand."

"You both are serious about each other, right?" she confirmed.

Hilda nodded. Colleen broke into a smile. Suddenly, she couldn't wait for what lied ahead.

***

Hilda was not scared and anxious about replacing her late husband anymore. She wanted a new beginning, and she knew Sam would desire the same for her.

Time has passed very quickly. Hilda and Tim had been married for almost a year now. Pastor Philips from the church that Tim attended, First Baptist Church of Tarrytown, married them under the giant maple tree by the lake.

It was a simple ceremony with only a few people from church and a picnic back at the farm. Love was in the air throughout the ceremony, and all the guests cheered and clapped for the newlywed couple.

Colleen had been delighted to help with preparing the food. The table was decorated with fresh ham, potato salad, string beans, lemonade, apple cider, and apple pies, but no wedding cake. It was a country wedding. There were checkered table covers and fresh daisies in mason jars tied with ribbons. Colleen hit the nail on the head with the decorations. It was the precise style her brother had wanted.

She was incredibly happy to be a sister-in-law to Hilda. Meg came to the wedding with her husband, Paul. Tim and Paul knew each other from church. They had both attended it for years. Tim had also known about Meg and that she was good friends with Hilda. "It indeed is a small world," Tim had said. He asked her out of curiosity, "Miss Judy and Mr. James are your parents, right?"

When she had nodded, he laughed, "It really is a small world. I know those two from church, too. Paul told me about them."

Tim turned to Paul, "I'm glad to see you came. You have gotten yourself a lovely wife. Speaking of wife...where's my bride?" Tim looked around to locate his wife and saw her speaking to some of the ladies from the church.

He caught himself smiling, noticing her full cheeks and sparkling eyes. She looked happy and healthy after overcoming her past anxieties. His heart could handle no more.

After the wedding ended, Hilda silently wept on her husband's shoulder. She sobbed, "I feel so free and happy now. It's almost scary. I can't wait to turn over a new leaf in my life with you." He lifted her chin with a delicate hand. He kissed her softly.

"I love you," they whispered to each other.

Even after a year passed since their marriage, they were still lovey-dovey. Hilda had stopped working at the diner because life at the farm was so busy but in a good way. She helped Tim around with his farming tasks and found comfort in living alongside nature.

Every morning, they started their day with coffee on the porch, and Tim read his bible to Hilda. She found her life to be tranquil and peaceful. She enjoyed watching the sunrise and preparing breakfast for them as her Mama did so many years ago.

Their lives were picture-perfect, and Hilda thought it couldn't get any better. For the first time in years, she was so satisfied. Just like any other day, the ham was sitting in the oven, warming up. Tim was waiting for the clock to strike seven. He had to wake Adal up for school. He could hear the cows starting to stir while Roger, a crazy old rooster, crowed in the distance.

"Time to wake up, sleepyhead," Tim said and kissed Hilda on the top of her head. After waking her up, he walked out but immediately reached for the doorcase to balance himself. Hilda got up, "Tim? Are you alright?"

"Oh yes, I just stood up too fast. You know how it is," he shrugged. Hilda didn't want to remind him that he had been lightheaded twice this week. It worried her. She was going to keep an eye on him. Colleen stopped by later that day as she did pretty much daily. But today, she brought a batch of cookies she and Lilly made from scratch.

Colleen was welcome to make herself at home any time, and she did just that. Colleen loved to cook and often made dinner for all of them. Tim enjoyed family time, so he never complained about Colleen visiting so frequently.

Hilda was also a great cook. She learned to cook from her Mama. She prepared plenty of German dishes whenever she could. She called Tim's favorite dish, 'Christmas dinner.' It was a dish that was made for special times, hence, its name. Hilda felt every day on the farm was special, so she insisted on making it more often.

"What's for supper?" Tim yelled from the yard.

"Christmas dinner," Hilda yelled back enthusiastically. His mouth watered, imagining that creamy bacon gravy poured over the chicken. "She's teaching me how to make it," Colleen shouted, making Hilda laugh. Adal and Lilly were setting the table. They were best friends, more like sisters now.

"Go wash up, girls," Colleen said. "Tim, come inside and get washed up, too. It's time to eat," she yelled through the window. Tim walked up on the porch with his overalls that were covered in manure. "Oh my! Tim, it is better for you to stay in the barn. I'll bring you some clean clothes. You stink like the cows," Hilda covered her nose. A fit of laughter ensued after her words.

"Sure, I'll go, but only after a nice kiss," Tim teased and puckered up his lips. Hilda rolled her eyes jokingly, "Get away, Timothy Kelly, or I'll…"

"What? Send me to my room?" He winked. Hilda shook her head, "Now, what am I going to do with you!"

He chuckled and turned toward the yard, dragging the hose to clean himself up. "I'll make the salad dressing while you take the clothes to him," Colleen said.

"Great. I'll be back quick," Hilda said. After Tim was all dressed up in neat clothes, the family clasped their hands and said their graces. Then, they gorged on the delicious meal. Once supper was over, the girls took the dishes over to the sink as Hilda and Collen washed them.

Hilda poured Tim some coffee and sat next to him. They joked around for a while till Tim began to stare at his hands. Hilda didn't say much at first, but he kept doing it. He looked as if he was thinking deeply about something.

Finally, curiosity got the best of her. "What's up with your hands?" She asked as she grabbed them. "Why do your fingers look so blue," Colleen chimed in. "I know. It must be that new mix of weed killer I bought," he explained.

"Well, don't use that anymore. Who knows what chemicals are in there," Hilda advised. They drank their coffee, then Tim went to the barn to settle the animals in for the night.

"How are things at the diner?" Hilda asked Colleen. "Same, you know…Old Ralphie comes in every morning for his regular breakfast of eggs and ham. He asks for you every time. I swear that man's losing his mind," she went on.

"Aww. He's so ornery most of the time, but sweet too." Hilda chuckled. They finished up the dishes and sat on the porch. Hilda asked Colleen if she had noticed that Tim seemed a bit tired. Colleen said, "Tim has been feeling fatigued more lately, but he just took on a new family. Maybe, it's just stress."

"Stress! I hope not, oh my," Hilda worried. Colleen glanced at the clock and realized it was time for her to leave. "Show yourself out when you are ready, but no hurry. I am going to check on Tim and get some chores done," Hilda excused herself and went to the barn to help Tim milk the cows.

She knew worrying too much was not good. As she entered the barn, she saw him singing Amazing Grace to Milly, the brown goat. She giggled in a corner, content that she married such a funny man. He was done with the milking, and all the animals had been fed and put up.

So, Hilda went to the garden to weed the tomatoes and pulled out some that had turned red. She then took the wheelbarrow and filled it with green beans. She wanted to get the beans canned in the morning and start on the beets and peas next.

Colleen gathered her things from the kitchen and fetched the girls. "Hey, Hilda? Hilda!" Colleen called to the garden for her friend. "Adal wants to stay over at my house with Lily. Is that okay?"

Hilda yelled back, "That's fine. Send her to her room to get some clean clothes. She needs a bath! She stinks like Tim." Collen let out a chortle.

"Bye, Mama. I love you," Adal yelled out. Tim jumped behind Adal and asked, "What about me?" He scooped her up and kissed her cheeks. "I love you too, daddy," she managed to say as she giggled from the tickles.

Tim and Hilda brought the beans to the porch and snapped them while listening to the radio. There was too much static on the radio, so they opted to just sit and talk. They loved spending time with each other. Hilda liked having a sister-in-law. Colleen and Lily were a part of their everyday lives. She couldn't imagine being any happier than she was right now.

"Do you mind that Colleen is here so much," Tim asked as he fiddled with his mug.

"Not at all," Hilda replied. "She's a great help. She always wants to do the cooking, so I get to spend more time with you and the girls."

"She can't cook as well as you, Hilda. That's a fact! My belly is so full I could burst," he laughed.

"That's because you ate too much. Come on, let's call it a night. My back is killing me," she sighed. "Thank you, Lord, for this day. I pray I was pleasing in your sight for all

I did today. Keep us all safe till morning. Amen," Tim prayed out loud.

"Amen," Hilda followed. She had started to pray and attend church because of Tim. She attended for a few days and found the experience to be quite soothing.

They both took a quick bath, then snuggled in bed. Tim kissed her on the forehead, and she pulled him closer. A year into their marriage, and they still loved each other like the first day.

Chapter 13
Sickness

Hilda reached over and saw that Tim was not lying next to her.

Tim had woken up in terrible pain. He thought his stomach would probably blow up. He was in the bathroom on the floor, shivering next to the toilet. He vomited for half an hour. Hilda heard the retching sounds as soon as she woke up.

"Tim. What's wrong?" she hurried toward the bathroom. The door was left ajar.

"I seemed to have eaten too much last night as you said," he managed to say between the vomiting.

She frowned, "I think you are working too hard. That is why you are getting sick. Tomorrow, I will do all the chores with Jimmy and Tommy. They will show me what to do."

Normally, Tim would not hear of any of this, and he would never allow Hilda to work in the barn or fields. But he was too sick to argue. He remained in the bathroom for a few more minutes while Hilda dipped a cloth in cold water for his head. She helped him lay back in bed. He was terribly weak and looked pale. She covered him with a light blanket. She stayed next to him the entire day, putting cool rags on his head and preparing warm meals for him.

When Roger fell asleep, she got up. She placed a water bottle and a plate of cubed fruit on the table. Tim was in a deep slumber. She went to the barn where Tommy and Jimmy, two young men Tim had hired a while back, were working. They were very loyal to him.

Hilda saw both working tirelessly without wasting even a second to wipe the sweat off their forehead. They were milking the cows and feeding the chicken. She told them about what happened and that she came out to help.

"No need, ma'am, we can manage. You tend to Mr. Tim. We got this," Tommy said humbly.

They had cleaned up and divided the main farming tasks amongst each other. They kept reassuring that she may return to Tim, and she obliged. She was grateful for their immense help. She went back inside and made him some tea and toast.

She blackened the toast just like her Mama did when she used to get sick. Mama told her that black toast cured a sick stomach. She took the toast and tea to him and tried to get him to eat. He managed to munch on some of it. He weakly mentioned that he felt somewhat better. She helped him change his clothes. Then, she slipped his arm above her shoulder to guide him to a chair.

He put his bible on his lap and started to read. Hilda prayed with him and then left the room for a bit to call Colleen.

"Can you keep Adal for a few days? Tim is terribly sick. I think it's the flu," she informed.

Colleen gasped, "Oh no, that's not good at all! You can't handle it all alone, Hilda! I am coming over."

Hilda breathed out in defeat because she knew Collen would show up anyways. Colleen always worried plenty for her family. She just called to ask Collen to keep Adal with her for a few days. But having some help didn't seem like a bad idea.

She replied, "Well, if you insist, but don't bring the girls inside..."

A few hours later, Colleen was sitting by the bed with chicken soup. She looked worried, knowing that Tim wasn't getting enough nourishment. She sat there and spoon-fed him the soup, even though he tried to push her hand away. Hilda watched as his condition seemed to get worse than before.

"That's it!" she said. "You're going to the doctor."

She pulled the pickup truck around the front and went to the barn to get one of the guys. Jimmy came out and helped them carry Tim to the truck. Tim didn't resist. Normally, he disliked hospitals with all his might. Right now, he seemed like a different person. It was shocking to everyone.

They drove to a nearby clinic. One of the doctors, Doc Baker, always recognized the couple as they often visited the clinic. He was a short and stubby guy with a friendly attitude. When they reached his office, Hilda left Tim in the truck and ran inside to get some help in carrying him.

Doc Baker came out himself. He took one look at Tim. With a look of concern and disturbance, he said, "Get this man to the hospital this instant. I'll call ahead."

Hilda drove him to the hospital, where they admitted him right away. He was diagnosed with exhaustion and flu. Once all the proceedings were done, Hilda drove back home to check up on the animals. All this time, her hands were shaking from fear and anxiety.

Colleen had called Meg to take care of the girls and stayed with her and. Hilda and Collen were so grateful for Meg's quick response.

Hilda called Eva to let out the frustration caused by the unforeseen situation. It was her habit to call Aunt Eva whenever something terrible or nerve-wracking happened. She had been worried sick ever since Tim had got admitted.

Eva calmed her down, "Honey, you get some rest, and I'll get there shortly. We will go to the hospital together tomorrow, okay?"

Hilda trudged toward her bed, exhausted, and fell fast asleep. Eva woke her up the next morning. They dressed up and drove directly to the hospital. When they arrived, they were met by the head nurse, Helen. Nurse Helen told them that Tim was alert and much better now.

They were still keeping him for a week to monitor him,

but he was going to be fine. Hilda went into the room and saw him sitting up. He was trying to convince the nurses that he needed to go home.

"Oh no, you don't!" Hilda shouted at him. "You scared me so much! You will do what the doctors say!"

"Yes, ma'am," he responded instantly and put his legs back under the blanket. Hilda made sure he completed his stay in the hospital until he was fully fit and healthy. He was there for a week but recovered his health in less than three days. He returned home and had to make up for the tasks left undone on the farm. He was thankful for Jimmy and Tommy, who did their part in helping around.

He was amazed that Hilda managed to get the early canning done. "I did a lot while you were lying around," she laughed. "Oh, is that how it is?" He teased and grabbed her, and kissed her face all over. Since Adal was not home, they took advantage of their time alone. They drowned in each other's eyes, savoring the intimate moment. They thought their lives were back on track again.

Chapter 14
Tim's Collapse

Meg came by the next morning with Adal. She had taken care of Adal while Tim was recovering. She instantly fell in love with the little girl who was so obedient and cheerful. She wanted to keep Adal at her place for a few more days.

"How is he doing?" Meg asked as soon as she entered the room. "Go in the barn and see for yourself. Good as new," Hilda replied with a smile. That was all Adal, who was eavesdropping hiding behind Meg's leg, had to hear. "Daddy, Daddy!" She screamed excitedly and ran toward the barn. She collapsed into his arms and gave him the biggest kiss and hug.

"Hey, doodlebug, I guess you missed me, huh?" Tim tapped her button nose. She had her arms wrapped so tightly around his neck that he had to loosen her grip to breathe. "I'll take that as a yes. I missed you too," he said and hugged her once more. He put her down, but she was still hesitant to let go. She grabbed his leg, hugging it. She put both of her feet on top of his boots, and he walked with her attached to him.

235

They laughed to their hearts' content. It seemed that all had returned to normal. Hilda also sneaked into the barn and loved the sight of her family, looking as happy as ever. Meg stayed for a while.

She and Paul had just bought a new house that cost them around $5,000. Hilda couldn't believe things could cost that much. She spent money cautiously after Sam's death because she had to raise Adal and keep the house expenses in check. The time she wasted thousands of dollars on unnecessary shopping was long gone.

Meg said that she and her husband were ready to start a family soon. But she was also scared at the same time. She saw what had happened to Hilda, and she had been reading up on what happened to some mothers after childbirth. Many studies showed that pregnancy could affect a woman's brain.

Doctors were apparently experimenting with electric shock treatments. Some doctors were saying that it was a disease that caused some women to kill their babies. Meg wanted to talk to Hilda about this issue, but she didn't know how to bring it up. So, she just didn't.

Hilda tried to reminisce about the days she, Colleen, and Meg were such close friends, but Meg didn't want to talk about it. Hilda found that to be odd. They laughed out loud in between the conversation at times, though. They remembered teaching Hilda how to apply makeup and teaching each other dance moves. They couldn't help but giggle at those memories.

About an hour later, Colleen walked in. "Helloooo, Meg," Colleen said cheerfully.

"Hi, I've been here for some time now," Meg replied and glanced at the clock. "Well, I have to go fix Paul some supper. I'm glad Tim is doing well, Hilda," Meg said and gave Hilda a tight hug, then walked right past Colleen. Hilda was bewildered to see her not greet Colleen. They could at least hug it out as Meg was leaving for home, but Meg's expression turned sour just seeing Colleen.

Noticing that, Hilda was reminded of her conversation with Meg after Colleen had come to her house and thrown a tantrum. Even at that time, Meg was fidgety, talking about Colleen as if she wanted to change the topic. Hilda didn't think much of it, but now, it was a little too obvious that something was going on.

Colleen went toward Hilda. She wasn't concerned that Meg brushed past her like a stranger. She said, "I brought some homemade iced lemonade for Tim. Where is he?"

Hilda replied quickly, "He's in the barn."

"Let's have some of the lemonade," Hilda added. She wanted to settle her raging thoughts for a while.

"Honey, do you know the price of these lemons? I made this just for Tim!" Colleen replied with a smirk. She took the thermos to him. Hilda shook her head to herself. She was probably overthinking it all. She pulled the roasted chicken out from the oven and put the rolls in.

Immersed in her thoughts, she drained the water from the potatoes and mashed them. Then she scooped the carrots from the chicken pan and set them aside. At last, she out everything in the oven to warm them up. After supper was piping hot and ready, she called Tim.

Tim came in as happy as a lark. He washed up and sat down at the table with Adal. Colleen and Lily had left as fast as they had come. Tim said his grace, and they ate together as a happy family.

"How was the lemonade?" Hilda asked.

"It was good, but why was she so stingy? There was barely a mouthful," he said.

Hilda lifted a brow, "Well, she said the price of the lemons was so high. I bet that could be it."

They then started to talk about Adal starting school soon. Adal was quite excited about her new journey. She couldn't wait to have a birthday party with all her friends, just like Lily.

After dinner, Hilda washed the dishes, and Tim and Jimmy went to the farm to take care of the animals. Hilda bathed Adal after finishing the house chores and dressed her for bed. Adal wanted Tim to read her the story tonight. The night ended on a good note with Tim recovering and their lives getting back to normal once again.

In the next few weeks, Tim and Hilda worked on getting the farm ready for winter, which would be upon them in no time. He was stocking the silo with grain for silage and stacking the bales of hay, making sure there was enough space for air circulation.

Tim had to repair the fences, fix a few stalls, and pull out the storm windows for the house. He was always so busy.

Hilda kept canning as fast as she could. The tomatoes were in abundance this year.

Hilda took Adal and Lily for berry picking, and they filled up several jars with homemade blackcurrant and blackberry jam. It was hard work, but Hilda enjoyed it. She loved everything about the farm. Gone were the days of fancy dresses, shoes, and purses! She had given them all to Eva because she needed them for work.

Tim was inundated with work and worried that he was overexerting himself. Hilda could tell. He was working hard, and he was afraid that he might not have recovered enough to be jumping right into the workload. His muscles were cramping up, and they had gotten red and swollen from lifting and sawing. She rubbed liniment on his aching muscles at night. That seemed to help him for the time being. She couldn't wait for him to be able to rest.

It was another day of labor and hard work. Tim was on the farm, and Hilda brought him an egg sandwich to munch on to regain some energy. "Tim? What is wrong?" She asked him immediately after seeing his hands. He shook his hands vigorously.

"My hands fell asleep again," he laughed.

"Why would your hands be sleeping?" She asked seriously. Tim could tell that she didn't understand what he meant. He found the language barrier funny sometimes. "They are not sleeping like snoring away, ha-ha. I feel a tingle in my hands. It's like the nerves are waking," he explained.

"Oh, Sclafende Finger."

He chuckled, "I guess, hey, it's okay! Happens to my legs, too. I'm just tired."

She was a little concerned, and he did need rest. She made him a nice cup of hot cocoa and sent him "up the wooden hill" as her father used to refer to the stairs. "Colleen has been coming every night. I'm going to ask her to stay here for a few nights, so you can rest," she told him.

"No, please don't. Then, I don't see Lily, and besides, she always has something yummy for us," he rolled his eyes.

"Such a baby you are! But I have to admit that blueberry pie was great, and her lemonade was perfectly sweet and tart. I'm glad she made enough for us a few days back," she said and gave him a huge kiss and whispered goodnight.

"I'm not THAT tired," he whined as he patted her butt.

"I'm dog tired. You get some rest now!"

He showed a tired smile, "Okay, ma'am."

He said his prayers and was out like a light. He woke up early, even before Roger. It was the pain that woke him up. His legs were hurting, and his arms were so painful that he couldn't lift them. "Hilda...Hilda...." he tried to wake her up. She was fast asleep. He went downstairs and drank some more of the lemonade Colleen made him ease his dry throat. He then read his bible and laid down on the couch to sleep some more.

Roger woke him. He stood up and felt a little shaky. He smelled the bitter coffee. He heard the sizzle of the bacon and eggs and the pop of the toaster. He washed his hands, kissed his beautiful wife, and expressed his gratitude to God through a short prayer. All that pain had him worried, but it flew away after passing a glance at Hilda. After being up for a bit, his muscles started to cramp up again. "Hilda, will you rub more liniment on my back and shoulders?" He asked as he drank some coffee.

"Sure, I'm also calling Dr. Baker today," she added.

"Aw, now don't make it such a big deal. I just overdid it this week, that's all."

"Dr. Baker can tell me that," she firmly replied.

He shook his head, and she shook the fork at him. They locked eyes and ended up smiling. Just then, they heard Adal call out, "Daddy!"

She ran to Tim. He ruffled her hair, "Good morning, doodlebug. Did you sleep well?"

She nodded gleefully. "Let's have some of mommy's terrific alligator toes and dinosaur fingers," he joked. Tim picked up his mug, and it fell right out of his hand. Coffee spilled all over him. Hilda ran over with a cloth and wiped it up.

Tim was puzzled by what just happened. He had barely any feeling left in his fingers, but he did not tell Hilda. He finished eating breakfast as best as he could. Thankfully, Hilda only scolded him and did not notice his numbness.

Tim stood up and cried out in pain. Hilda perked up, rushing toward him. She immediately made him lie on the bed, and she rubbed him down with liniment. His wrists were swollen, as were his ankles and toes. His fingers had a blue tint to them. She called Dr. Baker right away. The ambulance arrived after she described his condition. He was taken to the hospital and immediately admitted.

Hilda was frantic and worried, so she called Colleen. "Oh, Colleen, it's bad. They think he's been poisoned with some farming chemicals," she cried hysterically.

"I'll be there," Colleen reassured.

Eva came to the hospital to get Adal. Adal looked scared. She was on the verge of tears and told Eva that she didn't want to lose another daddy. Eva took her home while Hilda stayed with Tim. She was holed up in the room for hours, just staring at Tim, who lay unconscious. He was treated for his numbness, and the doctor had put him to sleep. He looked so peaceful.

Hilda felt her stomach grumble. She lifted herself up to buy a sandwich, but she noticed Tim's body starting to twitch. He was grabbing his chest in pain. Hilda could tell he was having a seizure, as she had once seen a family member suffer through the same.

She immediately ran to get a nurse. In a moment, the nurse ran into the room and pulled the curtains. Soon, a herd of medical personnel came running in. Hilda was pushed into the hall while she frantically screamed for her husband.

Colleen stood beside her, looking at the scene with horrified eyes.

Chapter 15
The Big Secret

Meg knew it was time to come forward and reveal this secret. She had carried it for far too long, and it weighed heavily on her. She prayed that her father would understand why she had not come forward sooner.

Colleen had done enough damage, and she needed to be stopped. It was high time. Meg had been held hostage to Colleen's threats and intimidations for too long. She was dreading what was to come, and it made her blood boil.

Meg walked into her father's office. He was on the phone, so she just sat on the wooden chair on the right side of his desk. Her mind went back to the many times she had visited her father as a little girl in his office. Not much had changed. The room still had the same desk, phone, chair, and the same nameplate that read 'Chief Det. James Foley, Homicide'.

His career as a detective was flourishing, and he had won many awards. He was instrumental in solving several high profile homicides throughout his career. He had started off as a rookie cop in New York City in 1930 when the mob was powerful and ruled the city. He learned how to identify people and unmask their true selves quite early.

He was smart and learned quickly. By listening and gathering intelligence, he made his way to the top. So, it was no surprise that Commissioner Valentine asked for him specifically when he started his Commission in 1934.

Foley was a quick learner, and being born and raised in the city made him street-savvy, proving helpful in his detective duties. However, he could not see that his own daughter Meg was in trouble, and she had been suffering for quite some time. She was proud of her father, and he was always proud of her. He didn't know that she was about to come up to him and unveil something that would change everything for many families.

"Yes, Commissioner... I'll get right on it, sir. I'll send Detective O'Brien in for an interview," Foley answered on the phone. He quickly added, "Yes, sir...he's one of my best..."

He kept talking and silently waved Meg in, who was lurking by the door. He was always busy. He worked day and night, and Meg often overheard many important phone calls over the years. Right now, she wanted to vomit and just couldn't think straight. She sat down and waited for his call to end.

"Detective O'Brien? This is Chief Detective Foley. I need you to interview that witness again on the Kelly case," Foley said as he attended another call. Meg's eyes widened at his words. Her ears turned red. She put her hands together to keep them from trembling. She had all sorts of thoughts running through her head. She wanted to leave, but she gritted her teeth and sat still.

"Yeah, that's the one. Colleen is his sister. She is downstairs at the front desk, waiting. She said she found out something and wanted to inform someone," He continued.

"I'm not sure, but I have a funny feeling about her. Keep her there for a bit. Yeah, that's right...you know what I mean. I have to go now. My kid is here to check up on the old' man..." Foley said. Funny how cops talked when they were at work, Meg thought.

He turned his chair toward her and asked nonchalantly, "Hey, what's the honor?"

"Dad?" she began. "I came down here with something to tell you."

"Why such a glum face? Did something happen?" he asked.

"Well ...sort of..." she stuttered.

"Meg, I'm your father, and you can tell me anything," he replied.

"Oh daddy..." she burst into tears. She may have been a grown woman, married, and settled down, but she was still her father's little girl. And she always kept herself composed in front of others but bawled in front of her father.

"I've kept a secret that I should never have, and it may have cost someone their life," she blurted out between teary hiccups.

Foley lifted a brow in confusion, "What are you talking about?"

"Does this have to do with your friends Colleen and Hilda?" he inquired.

She nodded right away.

His voice gained momentum, "You need to tell me right now!" He was more concerned than angry.

He never liked Colleen, but he had no real reason until now. It was just his gut. She came across as syrupy sweet. She used proper manners, and she was way too eager to please the people around her. Him being a cop, he could see right through her, but he had no reason to point fingers at her due to a lack of evidence. There was something off about Colleen.

He tried to tell Meg about this years ago when he caught them smoking outside a bar that the police were getting ready to raid. She was a regular at the bar, and it was recently exposed for fraud transactions. Colleen bawled her eyes out when she was interrogated, and she avoided his questions so swiftly. It made him believe she knew about the issue. He felt that she was involved in other dangerous plans, and it didn't sit well with him.

Meg was a follower, and Colleen was the troublemaker. Foley could tell by looking from afar. Meg had not been able to make friends easily, so he didn't say much. He monitored their relationship the best he could, and it was not easy as he had to work so much. His wife, Judy, was a full-time secretary at the church and had Meg involved in many church activities. They both never got to spend enough time with her together.

Meg was also close friends with Hilda, who at this very moment was under suspicion of murdering her first husband, Sam Granger, several years ago. She was also suspected of attempted murder by arsenic poisoning of her current husband, Tim Kelly. It had been a week since the case opened, and he was stressed about it, especially knowing it involved Meg's closest acquaintances.

"Hilda did not kill Sam, nor did she try to kill Tim," Meg mentioned as if she could hear her father's thoughts.

"And just how do you know this?" He said impulsively.

"Don't tell me! Are you involved? I knew that girl was no good. She didn't even want her own child. Did you know that? Imagine what kind of woman she is...both of them–" he was now pacing around the room and running his hands through his hair in worry.

"What? Dad, no!" Meg yelled. "It isn't what you think. Let me explain," she said and motioned for him to sit down. "I didn't do anything but kept a secret that I can no longer keep. I have to tell you, but I need you to listen. Okay? No cutting in," she pleaded.

He sat back down and entwined his fingers in front of him on the desk.

Meg began, "It all started a long time ago. You know Colleen and Hilda became my friends when we were in high school, right? Because I was so shy and well...I never fit in. Colleen was nice to me. Mom was always at church and telling me to be a good girl and believe in the Holy Spirit. 'Boys only want one thing, Meg,' she told me that sort of nonsense. No one would even look my way, Dad!"

"Meg..." he tried to get a word in, but she cut him off. "Just listen, please. This is not easy for me, and I have a lot to explain. Colleen showed me how to look pretty. She showed me how to flirt. She lent me clothes, so I didn't look like a nun," she stated.

"You never looked like a nun, and you had great clothes," he chimed in.

"Well, I looked plain and felt that way. Colleen knew how to catch the eyes of boys, and I wanted to be like her. She was fun. She made me laugh, and I felt good for a change. I was tired of being plain. She got everything she set out for, and I wanted to be like her. I hate to say it now, but I idolized her," Meg sighed out loud.

She looked down, "Hilda, too. Hilda was just as much of an outcast as me. She came from Germany without her parents and lived with an aunt that didn't really know how to parent her. Colleen took care of her, too. She was good for both of us. That was what I thought at the time. Colleen had nice clothes, wore makeup, and was popular with the boys. What 17-year-old doesn't want that?"

"I understand, but you know Mom and I were always there for anything that you needed, right?" Foley spoke softly.

Meg shook her head, "That's what you are saying, but you weren't. You both worked all the time. You provided for the family and did everything right but never noticed me. Dad, it's not your fault, but I need you to not think like that. I was 17. Now, I am married and see things differently. That's why I'm here. I need to fix the wrongs no matter what it costs me."

"Okay, I'm listening," he said, bobbing his head.

She glanced at him worryingly and then stared back at her trembling hands. "Colleen and I graduated together. Hilda dropped out because it was too much for her. Colleen eventually went to work with Hilda and me at the catering company.

Colleen told me that she was going to inherit a lot of money and that she would travel the world. She got pregnant right away with Lily and married John Logan. John was a soldier and sent to France. Sadly, he was killed in action," she explained.

"Yes, go on," he was listening but not liking it. It was taking too long.

"Well, she was forced to move in with Tim and their grandfather. She hated that farm. But she told me her grandfather was old. When he died, the farm would be left to her and Tim since Jason had passed away in Italy. She told me that she would get Tim to sell the farm, and she'd be set for life."

"But what about Lily?" He asked.

She closed her eyes in worry and said, "Tim adored Lily, and Colleen said that Tim would have no problem keeping

Lily while she was traveling. Oh, don't get me wrong. Colleen loves Lily and is a great mother. But when her grandfather died, he left Colleen little money and entrusted the entire farm to Tim. Colleen was livid! She told me she would get her fair share, no matter what."

Meg was trying to get it all out before she lost her nerve. "So? What happened?" he asked.

She went on, "Nothing. She couldn't get anything more because it was all done legally. Tim told Colleen he would never sell the farm because it was special to him. He felt guilty for not being able to serve as his brother and brother-in-law, especially since they never made it home."

Meg paused and cleared her throat. Then she continued in a raspy voice, "He told Colleen she could live with him on the farm forever if she wanted, but she refused and went to the city with Lily. She used the inheritance she received to buy a small apartment. She still needed to work, so she and Hilda continued to work at the catering hall. That was when Hilda met Sam, and I went to secretarial school in California for that year."

She rubbed her temples, "When I got back, Sam and Hilda had married, and Colleen was still working there."

Foley contemplated, "I remember when you came back. You were so stressed because you could not find a decent job. You moved in with Colleen and went back to working at the catering hall. I don't know why you wouldn't let me help you get a secretarial job..."

She interrupted, "Dad! Listen! There's a lot more. Hilda was having a blast with Sam. Hilda was hardly around. So, Colleen and I got really close. She and I shared many secrets. I have to tell you...well...okay, so when Hilda had gotten pregnant, all hell broke loose for her. She no longer felt the center of Sam's attention. She started to hang out with us again. We went out to shows, movies, shopping, and the funny thing is that Colleen always pretended she was broke, so Hilda always paid. Hilda didn't care about anything anymore. She didn't want a baby. It made her look like a bad mom."

She locked eyes with him, "Now, Dad, here is where it gets tricky. Colleen often told me how she hated the way Hilda was acting that no mother would refuse her own child. Of course, I agreed. Hilda was treating Sam awfully. It was surprising to me because they were so in love before she got pregnant. Colleen said she feared Hilda would 'turn Nazi' on him. What a thing to say! She said Hilda was more capable than we knew."

She drew a deep breath and gave a slight shrug, saying, "I just thought Colleen was being...you know, the typical Colleen. I didn't think anything of it. But one night after Adal was born, we'd been out to Copacabana. Hilda and Colleen were quite drunk. I don't drink. I learned my lesson years ago."

"I see," he remarked, urging her to continue.

Meg said, "Hilda confided in both of us that she wished Sam was dead, so she would have all the money and no headaches to deal with. She mentioned she had married him for money, to begin with, but fell in love with him for real. She said Adal had stolen Sam's affection. She had an odd sense of love, I thought."

"So? Did Hilda tell you she was going to kill Sam? Is that what this is all about?" he asked.

Meg quickly shook her head, "No. She didn't. She was drunk and spilling her feelings all over the table. That's when Colleen said that she knew someone who could help. I actually laughed. Both of them did, too. That was strange. It was never mentioned again."

"So? Then what happened?"

"Sam died in the car accident a few months later," she spoke in a low voice.

"And?"

"Colleen was there for Hilda, helping Hilda with her grief after Sam passed away. Hilda was in bad shape. We couldn't get her to eat, rest, or anything. She stayed in her nightgown all day. The nanny took care of Adal.

One night, when Colleen was home, we were still roommates at the time, she was drinking wine as usual. She ended up spilling the fact that she had helped Hilda. I asked her what she meant, and she said, 'You know, to get rid of Sam.' She also said that Hilda owed her now. I was flabbergasted!" Meg shook from fear just by remembering that bone-chilling moment.

Meg collected herself and continued, "Colleen told me she made the accident happen so that Hilda could be free, and Hilda owed her. She went on to say she set it up to look like an accident, but she had the brake line cut. Dad, I couldn't believe my ears. She told me Hilda knew nothing about it and wouldn't until the time was right. She said that she also set it up that if Hilda did not do her a favor, later on, she could pin the crime onto Hilda, and everyone would believe it."

"How?" He inquired at the speed of light. She had his full attention.

"That's what I asked her. Colleen told me that she had taken Hilda to meet Griff. Do you remember Griff, Dad? The young gas attendant at the Hanks Garage?"

"Yeah, that lanky guy, right?" He answered.

"Yeah, well, Colleen knew Hilda was good with cars. She had made sure people saw Hilda with them at the station while Griff worked on Colleen's car. Colleen told Griff how Hilda used to work in a garage with her dad.

Griff had known Sam, and he had met Hilda once before when Sam's car needed work. He was already aware Hilda knew about cars, so the setup Colleen had in mind was perfect. Colleen told me she had offered Griff $5,000 if he went to Hilda's house late at night and cut the brake line of

Sam's car. He had to keep his mouth shut. Colleen told Griff that Hilda wanted it done, but she didn't want to do it herself. It was all a lie to cover herself just in case."

Foley had a confused expression, "Why didn't you tell me all of this then? That incident was investigated by the uniforms, so we never got that case sent here. Why?"

He sounded annoyed. Meg explained, "Because I told you that Colleen and I had secrets. Dad, she had one on me, too! It's really going to be hard to hear. But let me finish. Colleen swore me to secrecy, or she would let my secret be known. Paul and I married, and I moved out."

"And then?"

Meg added, "Nothing more was said after Sam's death, so I thought maybe Colleen was making it all up to seem tough or something. She wasn't that truthful, so it would be typical of her to something like that. The fact that she often told the truth when drunk made me believe it, though. Hilda then met Tim through Colleen. She was finally happy. She seemed to be enjoying the new family life."

Sweat beaded her forehead, and she wanted to stop talking, as letting this all out made her feel so tired and lethargic for some reason. These were secrets she hid for such a long time. They were out in the open now. The burden had been lifted, but she felt so exhausted by it all.

"She still went over to their place regularly and loved to help cook them meals. No one questioned Colleen's motives because she was always so nice to everyone. Colleen even had Hilda bamboozled, but I know the real Colleen," Meg's voice shivered as she squeezed out the last words.

"I told you long ago..." he tried to interject.

"I know, Dad, but that's not the point now," she responded. "Over the years, neither Hilda nor I ever met Tim. It seems strange now. But as I think about it, Tim was the entire center of it all. It was all about money. When Tim started to get sick, Hilda was truly worried. She sent him to several doctors. Their diagnosis was stress or overworking. I wasn't until she took him to Beth David Hospital recently, and they found out he was poisoned. I knew then Colleen was at the bottom of this."

Meg felt like crying as she continued, "She said Hilda 'owed' her for the favor that Hilda never asked her for in the first place! She knew that Hilda could never hurt Tim, no matter how much she convinced her. So, she was sure she had to poison him herself.

She's a cold woman, Dad! She said she had been gradually increasing the dose over the months. She had intended to tell the police today that she suspected Hilda. She was planning on telling that Hilda confessed to her that she killed Sam, so any denial by Hilda would be unbelievable."

"Wow, so why did you not tell me this before so it could have been prevented? What's your secret that could be exposed?"

She gulped, "She threatened to tell you that I never went to secretarial school in California. I never went to school at all. That's why I was unable to let you help me find a job."

"So THAT'S the big secret? You could have told us..." he rambled on.

"No, Dad. I went to California with the money you gave me for school to have a baby. I had a baby, and I gave him up for adoption," she began to sob. "He'd be about nine now," she managed to get out. His mouth was left agape, and he blinked a few times in disbelief. He said with a trembling voice, "I'm sorry you held that in so long. What about the father of the baby?"

Meg wiped her tears, "I don't know. I gave up drinking entirely because that's how I conceived my son. I was drinking foolishly. I was 19 and stupid! I knew you and mom would be so ashamed. I went to Colleen, and she made arrangements with a cousin in California to help me out. She held this over my head forever. I was her prisoner. But now, I am done."

Just then, a light breeze blew into the room from the window slid open a little. It calmed the gripping tension in the room momentarily. Both father and daughter sat in silence and stared at each other. Their eyes gleamed with a sense of determination. It was time to purge the evil that had persisted amongst them for so long.

Chapter 16
Murder

James Foley was a father and a detective. He could not wrap his brain around the fact that he had failed at both. How could it be that Meg had needed him, and he did not know? How did he miss the clues on the Kelly case? It was quite obvious that he needed to scramble and fix this whole thing before it got worse.

Meg had left after crying and baring her secret to her father. She was finally relieved. She had been carrying such a burden for so long. What she told him had broken him a little, but he had to bear it all for now. He had a murderer to catch.

Detective O'Brien was interviewing Colleen at the station. Foley knocked on the door and asked O'Brien to step out. He told O'Brien all the information that he had heard from his daughter. The source was trustworthy as Meg was not only one of Colleen's closest friends but also the daughter of a top detective. So, she wouldn't lie.

"I can keep her talking while you get the search warrant, boss," said O'Brien.

"Nah, I'm going to go meet with Hilda and see if I can get her consent first. It will save a bunch of time. Get Colleen's written statement and have her sign it. Then let her go," Foley stated.

"Let her go?" O'Brien inquired, raising a brow.

"Yes, we don't have enough proof yet. No worries, I'll assign a uniform to keep a close eye on her," he replied and marched off.

Foley went straight to Beth David Hospital, where he knew Hilda would be. As he reached the hospital and came into the room, he saw Hilda sitting next to Tim. She was holding his hand while he was asleep in the hospital bed.

Tim had had a major seizure, and things were looking grim. He looked pale. His lips and fingers appeared blue. The detective was almost sorry he had to interrupt. Hilda was reading *23 Psalms* to Tim, which was one of his all-time favorites.

"Mrs. Kelly?" he said.

"Yes?" she replied in a low voice, her brows furrowed in confusion.

"I'm Chief Detective Foley of the New York City Police. May I have a word with you?" he asked, ensuring that his tone was sympathetic.

"Of course. How may I help you?"

Now, Foley was an experienced detective and didn't want to allow all of the information to slip through his lips. "I'm here to help you find out why your husband is so sick. We were informed that your husband, Timothy Kelly, has ingested massive amounts of arsenic. Do you know anything that can help us in this investigation?"

He had asked this phrase a million times in his career, and the usual answer was 'no.' Hilda, too, firmly denied knowing anything related to Tim ingesting arsenic.

Hilda said he had been complaining of headaches and stomach and muscle cramps for over a month. She insisted him to see several doctors until they could find out what was wrong with him.

"They were all saying he worked too hard and needed rest. Although that is true, sir, I know Tim was not himself.

Something was wrong," she explained.

Foley carefully added, "Mrs. Kelly, it would be helpful if you gave us permission to look through your house to see if we could find anything that may help us figure things out and save your husband." He knew he didn't really have enough for a search warrant, so consent from the owner was vital.

"Sir, you may do whatever you need to save my Tim," Hilda responded quickly. She signed the consent form as soon as he handed it to her.

With the signed document in hand, he drove back to the station and met with Detective O'Brien and Detective Murphy. He tapped them on the shoulders, "Let's go, boys, we got work to do."

Detective Murphy was an excellent photographer. He was a bit of an odd fellow, but he knew his craft. He immediately clicked several photographs of the Tarry Town Farm called 'Red Top Farm' as they arrived at their destination. He was particular that nothing be moved or touched until he captured it on his camera.

The flash of his camera going off was almost blinding. Detective O'Brien, on the other hand, made a rough sketch of the house and noted anything of significance into his drawings. When they searched the home, they knew they were looking for anything that could be connected to Tim getting poisoned.

They tossed drawers, closets, beds, and hampers. They even checked under sinks and pockets of hanging coats. They were careful not to make too much of a mess because Hilda was cooperating with them, and she was not actually the suspect. If they went by a search warrant, they could flip the place upside down for evidence, which was currently not the case.

While the other detectives were busy in the living room, Foley scrambled through the contents in the pantry. There were spices, seasonings, nuts, beans, and so much more. He grabbed a can of beans and saw a can filled with coffee beans of the brand 'Chase and Sandborn' behind it. It was open, unlike the rest of the cans. He opened the lid and saw a box of rat poison named 'Rodine Rat 'stuffed inside.

"Hey, come here! Look at this!" he shouted. The two detectives hurried toward him. Murphy photographed the box, and O'Brien placed it in a paper bag for evidence. They found various other items, as well. There were pajamas with vomit residue, bowls with a residue of poison placed in the sink, half-drunk jug of lemonade that smelled terrible. They documented it all and grabbed the evidence.

Foley left the detectives to explore the rest of the house and went back to his office and tapped out a search warrant for Colleen's home in Yonkers. A few hours later, he came with a signed search warrant in hand. O'Brien and Murphy arrived at Colleen's apartment, too. They knocked on the door and shouted, "Police with a search warrant, open up!"

They suddenly heard someone tripping and falling inside. Sounds of someone crushing plastic bags and stomping around could also be heard as if they were in a hurry. They decided to break open the door. They all rushed inside and headed toward the kitchen, where they heard someone dumping a liquid down the sink. They saw Colleen pouring out a box of the same poison that they found a few hours ago.

"Get out of my house!" She yelled at them. They went up to her to grab her. She kicked the officer as he approached, then threw a glass at him, which shattered into pieces and cut his arm. Other officers joined in.

She spat on them, bit them, and screamed, "You flatfoots are going to pay!"

Eventually, she was placed in handcuffs and forced to sit on the sofa while an officer was assigned to guard her. She was a tough one to handle. Officers left the house with bite marks and bruises all over their arms. One even needed stitches from the glass shards.

Foley had not expected her to resist so much. Repeating the same sequence of photo taking and sketch documentation, the search for further evidence began. They discovered an empty box of 'Rodine Rat Poison' in her trash bin. It had been wrapped up in a linen towel with a soiled pair of white gloves.

As they dug deeper into the trash, they found a spoon with white powder residue. They scrapped as much of the poison they could from the sink and packaged it, and they also took the box it came from. They even took swabs from Colleen's hands before they made her wash them for her safety.

In the bedroom, under her vanity chair cushion, they located a book on poisons and their effects. All were confiscated and collected as evidence. Colleen was placed under arrest for assaulting the police, destruction of evidence, and attempted murder of her brother, Tim. They transported her to the police station.

She met with Detective Foley in the interrogation room. "Colleen Logan?" he asked her.

She remained silent, staring sullenly at him. Her hair flowed every which way, and she had a scratch across her left cheek and a bloody nose that had been taken care of.

"Colleen, do you know who I am?" he asked.

She still would not speak. She motioned for a cigarette. Her face had a scowl that could kill.

"I am Chief Detective James Foley," he introduced himself.

"You're Meg's father!" she snapped. "I know who you are! All holier-than-thou! The lot of you!"

"Why do you say that?" Foley tried to understand her.

"Meg could never live up to your expectations and live her life as a pet of the church," Colleen screamed at him. Her words hit home, but he had to do his job and not get personal.

O'Brien was sitting at the end of the table. Foley called out to him, "Get Mrs. Logan a cup of coffee and undo those handcuffs, so she can have a cigarette."

O'Brien removed the cuffs but did not want to leave the room. "Sir, she's insane. She bites the skin out of people. Sir, she's no lady! See?" He showed her teeth marks on his arm.

Foley chuckled to himself, thinking how this small-framed woman took on six cops by herself and left marks on their skins.

"It's okay, O'Brien. The uniforms are right outside the room."

"So, anything else I can get you?" He asked after lighting her cigarette.

"Nope," she spat. "But I've got something to tell you," she blew smoke in his face.

"Really? What?" Foley snapped back, knowing she was going to rat out Meg.

"Meg, your darling Meg..." she blurted with an evil smirk on her face.

"Oh, you mean about the baby?" He cut her off.

"You know?" She was shocked enough to almost choke on her own smoke.

"Yes, and I know the entire story, so if you feel like telling your side, I'm here to listen, or do you want a lawyer?"

Colleen knew there was no way out of it now. Her only concern was Lily. "I don't want no stinkin' lawyer! I want to know what's going to happen to Lily." Her brows pulled together.

He shrugged, "Well, that's up to you, but I just heard that Timothy is recovering well. He will be fine soon. He's up and walking around today. I'm sure he'd love to take her. Right now, she is with Mrs. Brizzie, who volunteered to care for both girls for a while until Timothy and Hilda get back to normal."

"The farm?" she asked.

"I'm not sure why you would care, but Tim is a good Christian man and helped so many people. They have all taken it upon themselves to pitch in and help. Greed never pays, Colleen," he stared at her grimly. She lowered her head.

"But why, Sam? I can't quite understand why you killed Sam. Is there anything else you want to tell me?" He needed to know her precise motives.

"The cops are at Hank's Garage, removing the cut brake line from Sam's rusted car, and Griff has already confessed," he told her.

She rolled her eyes, "Hilda was the perfect muse. She was selfish and a terrible mother. Everyone gossiped about how she treated Sam. Then, one day, when we were out, she said she wished he were dead. That got me thinking...I could help her, and she could help me, you know?"

Leaning closer, Colleen said in a low voice, her tone was almost conspiratorial, "I didn't have a plan just yet, but if I got her to owe me, that would be good in the future. It's always good to have people owe you favors. So, I figured out how to do her a favor and bank one for me."

She tapped her cigarette on the ashtray and said, "But I needed to be smart in case Hilda refused. I knew no one liked her, and it was believable that she was capable of it, should someone question that it was not an accident. So, I set up the deal with Griff. I didn't know he was a stool pigeon."

"We already spoke to others who confirmed Hilda was no mother, but no one believed Hilda would kill Sam. We also asked about you, and many people thought you were not as saintly as you wished people to believe. What I don't get is why you would want her to kill Timothy, your own brother?" he asked.

She clicked her tongue and explained, "He's my brother, and I didn't want him dead at first. I thought he would leave the land once he got married, but I realized that he was obsessed with the place. I visited him frequently to convince him to leave that damn place and let me receive my share of land."

"But?" the detective raised a brow in question.

Colleen slapped her palm on the table and said, "But he was not budging! I wanted him to get married and settle down, but he was getting in my way. So many years, and yet, he was selfish enough to not even give me a piece of that stupid land."

She threw her hands up in the air. "I had no other option. He wouldn't sell that place. I wanted Hilda to be blamed, so I would get everything! She would be in jail, and I could sell that damn place! I only got enough to buy my apartment and pay for Lily's school. That's not fair!! He was the only one who wanted that filthy farm, and Grandpa knew it!"

Foley saw her face turn red with rage but remained silent, urging her to continue with a swift nod.

She went on, "How was I to know Hilda would really love Tim and would become the mother of the year! I didn't see that coming? I knew then that I had to do it myself. I had to go there regularly and pretend that I liked it. I had to be the perfect sister so that no one would suspect me. I made sure the stuff only went in Tim's food, not anyone else's like his lemonade glass, his piece of the pie, his bowl of soup…"

"What stuff?" the detective threw in a question.

She scoffed, "The poison! Don't be daft, detective; you know what I mean."

"I just want to be clear," he responded. "Were you concerned that Lily would accidentally ingest some of it?" He added.

Colleen snapped, "Of course! Boy, you are stupid, aren't you? I was afraid the girls would get hurt, so I brought it back and forth from my house. I put it in the coffee can and placed it at the back of the pantry. My plan would have worked if not for Meg. That sniveling shit! I suspected she told you because she refused to answer her phone. I left several messages with Paul, and she never called back. So, I knew she was avoiding me."

"Where is the poison now?" he asked.

"Find it yourself!"

"Where did you buy it?" he questioned her again, considering he needed to get out as much information from her as possible.

"Where do you think?" she spat.

"Well, Colleen, It looks like we are done here. Is there anything else you would like to add to your statement?" he added.

She waved a hand for him to leave.

He said and trudged toward the door, "Okay, the typist will have this ready for you to sign shortly."

He turned around, "O'Brien, escort Mrs. Logan to cellblock B, please."

***

Meg was avoiding Colleen for weeks now. She recently stopped answering her calls altogether. Knowing Colleen was nothing but evil; she was scared to death of what the woman was capable of.

Meg told her husband, Paul, the entire truth, even the part of her giving away the baby. She then went to break the terrible news to Hilda. She had wanted to tell Hilda for a long time, intending to ask for forgiveness. Paul went with her for support and safety.

They arrived at the hospital a few days later to find Tim walking toward them in the hall. "Praise the Lord! What a sight to see!" Paul said.

Paul and Tim had developed a good friendship through the First Baptist Church of Tarrytown. That was also where Meg met Paul. Tim had been attending the church for over 20 years, and so did Meg until she fell away due to the guilt of her sin.

"Look at you, ready to chase your ducks and stuff your cattle!" Paul chuckled. "Good to see ya, Paul," Tim beamed. Paul contemplated and said, "Meg needs to speak with you both. You feeling up to it?"

Tim smiled, "Sure, anytime. You guys just stop over the farm. I'll be leaving this place soon enough. I'm finally over this awful flu and getting my strength back."

No one had told him anything yet. Paul and Meg caught on. Meg hesitated but blurted, "Hilda, let's get a coffee and let the boys catch up."

Hilda was sitting on one of the waiting benches. She went along with Meg across the street to the Village Diner for a cup of coffee.

"Black, please," Hilda said to the waiter.

"I'll have just cream," Meg added.

They sat in front of each other in silence for a good ten minutes. "How are you holding up?" Meg broke the ice and reached across the table to hold Hilda's hands.

"I'm alright, but it was poison, Meg! The police have searched my house!" She exclaimed.

"I know," Meg said. "Dad told me," she caught herself saying.

"How could he get poisoned?" Hilda was so worried. "The doctor said this might have long term effects because it never really leaves your body. Your dad came to see me here and needed to ask me questions. I received a call from him half an hour ago, and I have to meet him at the station. But I don't want to leave Tim," Hilda grabbed her head.

She then pleaded, "Meg, would you and P…"

"Not another word. We will stay as long as you need us to," Meg reassured.

"Okay, I should go now, I believe. I'll be right back."

Hilda left the café, relieved that at least Tim wasn't alone, and Meg would stay by him. He still didn't know anything, and she didn't want him to panic in any way about her whereabouts. Meg would handle it all for sure. She hurried toward the station by grabbing a taxi. She rushed inside and met with Detective O'Brien. "I was supposed to see Chief Foley," she told him.

"You will, but first, I need to take a statement from you," he informed.

"A statement for what?" she asked nervously.

"Come in here and have a seat," he motioned for her to enter a very plain grey room with one window, a wood table, two chairs, and a cloud of heavy cigarette smoke. The smell of smoke was awful. She waved her hands to fan the smell. "Sorry, the lady before you smoked a lot. She was here a while," he apologized and opened the window to let fresh air in.

"Thank you. Now, what am I to tell you?"

"I'm here to help you find out what happened with your husband. We were informed that your husband, Timothy Kelly, has ingested poison. Do you know anything about that?" He began.

"Chief Foley asked me the same question. I don't know anything. Detective, how would I know about the poisoning?" She questioned.

"How's your marriage?" he asked.

"It is great. I love Tim very much. He's a good man," she was taken aback by the sudden question.

"Have you been married for a long time? And is this your first marriage?"

"What does this have to do with my husband?" she politely asked, truly wanting to understand.

The detective justified, "These are standard questions. They will help me clarify things."

He interrogated, "Now, tell me about your first marriage. Sam, wasn't it? What happened?"

She sighed out loud. "Oh my, such a long story, but I will tell you if it will help Tim," she said and described her life with Sam from the moment they met to his death. She stopped in between and thought for a minute.

"Go on, Mrs. Kelly, you're doing great," the detective said.

She choked back tears, "I hated myself. When I finally realized that I was a fool, Sam died in a car accident. It was all my fault. I killed him."

The detective's ears perked up, hearing that. "What did you say?" He questioned.

"I wished him dead. I didn't really want him to die. I was angry and wished something so silly," she cried hard.

"So, did you do anything to cause his death?"

"Yes, I wished it," she sniffed.

"Who's Griff?" He asked in an attempt to get to the

bottom of her claim.

"Griff is the mechanic that used to work on Sam's car," she informed.

"Did you know him personally?'

"Like, how do you mean?" She replied, not understanding where he was going with that.

He clarified, "Did you have lunch with him? Did you hang out with him? Was he your friend?"

"No, he was actually Colleen's friend. They were together sometimes. He just fixed my husband's car."

Another question came her way, "So, you never dated him?"

She felt insulted, "No! I was not a good wife, but I was never unfaithful! I loved Sam! I want to talk about Tim! What do you need me to do?"

"I'm sorry that I hurt your feelings, but I must ask about everything. Did Colleen dislike Sam? Did she offer to hurt Sam?"

The interrogation continued. Hilda was clear on her stance that Colleen had no ill feelings toward Sam, and she treated him with respect just as Meg. They talked about that one night, Hilda was drunk and angry and wished for Sam's death. And then came the question about the poison. Hilda remembered that they kept poison in the barn to take care of the mice.

"Who cooks your dinners?" Detective O'Brien pestered further.

"Well, I do, but Colleen also likes to cook. She brings Lily to play with Adal, and she often makes us soup, meat pies, fruit pies, and lemonade, all that stuff."

"Does she make things just for Tim?"

Hilda saw the big picture now, "Yes, she does! She told me she made him supper because he was sick. She couldn't possibly, oh, my God!"

She stood up and put her hands over her mouth.

The detective pushed back his chair, "I'll go get the chief for you."

Chief Foley came and rubbed Hilda's back to comfort her. "Hello, Hilda, this is a grave shock, isn't it?"

"Yes, I don't know what to think. Her own brother!?" She said in disbelief. He decided to inform her about everything starting from the financial troubles Colleen faced using Hilda as a pawn to accomplish her dirty deeds.

Hilda couldn't grasp that Colleen could be so vile. She immediately fainted. Only the image of Tim and Adal circulated in her head. She also felt so terribly bad for Lily that her chest tightened with pain.

She awoke to see Chief Foley beside her and a cold rag on her forehead. "I'm glad you're back with us," he sighed in relief. "Let's get you to your husband. We have to tell him."

"Where's Colleen?" She asked with fear.

"She and Griff are locked up. She felt no remorse about her actions, and she didn't apologize for her crimes. Both of them will be in there for a long time," he assured her.

Hilda felt dizzy from the anxiety. She collected herself and went back to the hospital. Hilda asked Meg and Paul to stay, even though they both felt ashamed. Hilda and Tim thanked them for all the help they did to solve this.

A nurse came from behind and drew open the curtains.

She said, "I've got great news. You can go home and recoup there. I'm throwing you out, and I don't want you back."

She pointed at Tim in a joking way, who had been a handful for all nurses as he hated hospitals and whined about leaving often. He burst out laughing, followed by snickers from everyone in the room.

Laughing out loud felt so weird and foreign after spending a day full of betrayal and backstabbing. But Hilda still broke into a smile, happy that all the demons dragging her down were finally caged.

Chapter 17
Home

When Tim and Hilda arrived home from the hospital, they saw several cars parked outside that they didn't recognize. They exchanged a confused look.

"What in the world?" Hilda said. She ran toward the house with Tim trailing behind.

There were people pulling up grown vegetables and preparing them for canning. Some ladies were boiling the jars, and some were cutting up the carrots, shelling the peas, snapping the beans, and blanching the ripe tomatoes. Some were pickling the beets and cucumbers.

The men were cleaning out the stalls, pitching hay, milking the cows, feeding the animals, washing and brushing all the horses, and completing the essential farm chores.

Tim recognized these people from church. He was dumbfounded to see them all here, working so tirelessly around his house. Hilda saw Mrs. Brizzie hanging out the sheets and washing clothes.

Eva and Mrs. Murphy were pitching in wherever needed. And Adal and Lily were running around with more jars, baskets of vegetables, and small buckets of water.

"What is this?" Hilda called out to one of the church ladies. The woman turned to her with a sympathetic look on her face. She took Hilda's hands and addressed the couple,

"We apologize for barging in like this. We all heard about what happened. Mr. Tim, we are praying for you. You're a good man, and you have always been the first to help those in need. So, now you need us. Please, go inside and rest up. Mrs. Hilda, your family, has been waiting for you. God bless."

Tim was moved to tears. "Wow...I am such a lucky man," he wept. After hearing what had happened, Tim was furious but mostly sad and disappointed. He felt lost and discouraged during the last day of his hospital stay. Many thoughts circulated in his head and all of them consisted of Colleen, the root of everything that went wrong in their lives.

He was more concerned about Lily, who was still too young to bear this tragedy, so he had to collect himself quickly. He needed to recover and bounce back from this dark place for the children.

Tim wiped his tears and saw Paul standing beside him with a smile on his face. Tim buried his head in his shoulders and silently cried, then leaned on Paul to go inside.

As he entered the living room, he saw flowers, cards, and gifts from the church people. He was overwhelmed with their generosity. All throughout the next week, these church members came by and helped around the house. It was a great week with everyone coming and going and helping out. It took the attention away from the tragedy, and it was nice to be back home.

However, it was hard on Lily because her mother was suddenly not around. Tim was honest and compassionate. She was a mature girl for her age, and he knew she would be okay. At least, Colleen had the decency to give Lily to him to raise without putting up a fight.

Tim and Hilda sat on the porch. They had just tucked the girls in bed. Hilda made iced tea. Even though Tim preferred lemonade, but he never wanted to see it again. They talked about Colleen throughout the night.

"I forgive her, Hilda. Not forgiving would only hurt us, so I forgive her. She is where she needs to be, which is prison. It will be hard on Lily, but she will be fine with us. God will make sure of it. I love you, Hilda," Tim let out his feelings. He caressed her cheek and whispered, "You have been great. I love you so much."

Hilda leaned in, smiling at his words. "I love..." she didn't get to finish as a car pulled up at their house. They looked down from the balcony to ease their curiosity about the sudden visitor. A soldier stepped out.

With widened eyes, Hilda stood up and shouted, "Zeke!"

The man looked up and waved enthusiastically, "Hildie!"

Tim stood up to greet him. He could recognize who Zeke was from his attire and the way Hilda greeted him. He said, "You must be Sam's brother. I've heard great things about you."

They invited him into the house, poured him a warm cup of coffee, and they all sat together by the balcony. Hilda turned to Zeke with a concerned face, "Zeke, sit down. My God, the war has been over for so long, and no one heard anything. Where have you been?"

He chuckled a little, scratching his head as if thinking of where to begin. He began, "I was hit hard in Italy during the Anzio battle. I was out cold. A man named Jason Kelly pulled me to safety as the line was hot with enemy fire. He never even batted an eye at the danger unfolding in front of us. He just pulled anyone hit to cover and held the line. I don't remember all of it, but I can tell you Jason saved many of us that day."

His eyes sparkled as he talkedabout this person. "He was the best buddy a man could ever have. I found out that you were his brother," he pointed toward Tim.

He continued, "I wanted to bring you his stuff in person and tell you how much he was loved, but I was in a hospital in Italy and then had to stay in England for so long. Sometimes, I didn't remember who I was."

He took his hat off and showed a huge indentation on his skull. He tried to make light of the situation. "Hard noggin' the Granger boys have," he chuckled.

Hilda stared at him in worry, but she was glad that he made it back safely. Zeke touched his head, feeling the gap in his skull, "I had no idea where I was from. They told me my name and stuff, but I didn't want to come home without memory. I learned of Sam's accident and that you had gotten remarried. I never met Adal. Is she as pretty as you, Hildie?"

She finally broke into a smile, "Oh, Zeke, you make me blush."

"Where are you staying?" she asked.

He thought about it, "I don't know yet. I'll probably stay at the Carson Inn."

"Nonsense! You stay right here," Tim said firmly. "The girls share a room, so we have an extra."

Zeke smiled gratefully at their kindness and decided to take them up on the offer. He talked with Tim about his brother, and they reminisced about memories that seemed to be locked up for long.

After a while, he turned to Hilda, "Oh, Hildie, I know Sam would be happy you are doing so well."

"Yes, I know he is good now with the Lord. After all these years, I finally know what success is. It certainly doesn't come from objects," Hilda replied.

It took so long, but Hilda finally didn't feel any burden on her shoulders. It was as if she were free at last. Nothing tied her down to the ground, and she felt light like she hadn't in a long time. She was finally a part of a happy family now.

As the clock struck 12, everyone went to their rooms to rest up. Hilda and Tim went to bed as well. They lay their in silence, listening to the crickets chirping.

"Tim? How many beds can we get in the girls' room?" Hilda asked all of a sudden.

"Oh, they are fine with that double they have. They like sharing," he replied with a laugh.

"No, not a bed. I was thinking of a crib," she said and looked at him lovingly.

"What would we need a cri..." he trailed off.

"Tim, we are going to have a baby!" Hilda said, her eyes lighting up.

Tim jumped up in shock. He turned to Hilda and grabbed her in a bear hug. "Oh, my God!" he said in a voice that shook with emotion.

Hilda could only laugh at his flushed face. She had a new doctor this time, and he specialized in "baby blues." They discovered new things about what happens during pregnancy, but Hilda was more than ready this time. She wasn't scared or frustrated with carrying a child within her anymore. Instead, she wanted to bear Tim's children. She wanted to give him a child that had both of their traits and features because she loved him so much. Also, she was not foolish and selfish anymore.

That night, she couldn't sleep at all, and she didn't know why. She turned to her right and saw Tim snoring away, which calmed her. She looked outside and saw the star twinkling like glass beads in the sky, and she again felt tranquil.

She wondered if one of them was Sam and that he was proud of her for finally letting go of all that hurt her. Her parents crossed her mind, and she remembered how she had never received a response from them. The desire to reunite with them still burned deep within, and this time, she wanted to reach out to them. She still had time.

Hilda remembered how she was before – the young and naïve teenager who had such high hopes from this country.

She had a German accent as thick as the fog that threw her under the bus every time she opened her mouth. She also recalled the relentless bullying that made her quit her studies once and for all.

One by one, Hilda recalled all the events that had led to this moment where she lay silently and peacefully with her loving husband. Everything had to go wrong first for things to turn right. And a small part of her still felt guilt, but hope was slowly taking over.

Drawing closer to Tim, she put her arms around him and buried her face in his chest.

Warmth…love…happiness….she had it all now. Finally, after all these years, she felt safe.

HOLLIE TUTRANI